ALBERT ANGELO

B. S. Johnson (1933–1973), an admirer of
Joyce and Beckett, was a novelist whose works combine
verbal inventiveness with typographical innovations. His books
include *Albert Angelo* (1964), *Trawl* (1966), *The Unfortunates*
(1969) and *House Mother Normal* (1971).

Also by B. S. Johnson

NOVELS

Travelling People

Trawl

The Unfortunates

House Mother Normal

Christie Malry's Own Double-Entry

See the Old Lady Decently

POETRY

Poems

Poems Two

SHORT PROSE

Street Children
(*with Julia Trevelyan Oman*)

Statement Against Corpses
(*with Zulfikar Ghose*)

Aren't You Rather Young to be Writing Your Memoirs?

ANTHOLOGIES
(*as editor*)

The Evacuees

All Bull: The National Servicemen

You Always Remember the First Time

MISCELLANEOUS

Well Done God!: Selected Prose and Drama of B. S. Johnson
(*edited by Jonathan Coe, Philip Tew and Julia Jordan*)

B. S. JOHNSON

ALBERT ANGELO

WITH AN INTRODUCTION BY

TOBY LITT

PICADOR

First published 1964 by Constable

First published by Picador 2004 as part of an omnibus edition

This edition published 2013 by Picador
an imprint of Pan Macmillan
20 New Wharf Road, London N1 9RR
Associated companies throughout the world
www.panmacmillan.com

ISBN 978-1-4472-0037-6

5 7 9 8 6 4

A CIP catalogue record for this book is available from the British Library.

Printed and bound by CPI Group (UK) Ltd, Croydon, CR0 4YY

INTRODUCTION

There's a shock coming up. A big, glorious, true shock. It's at the bottom of page 163.

Do not look at page 163 – at least, not until you've read the following paragraph:

If you want to receive *Albert Angelo* as B. S. Johnson would have wanted you to receive it, and as I would prefer you to receive it, then start with the Beckett epigraph and let page 163 happen to you when it does.

To those of you who have already skipped ahead to page 163 and returned to here: *Welcome back to the present. Welcome back your usual condition of avoiding big, glorious, true shock by checking, in advance, to see – click – what that shock might consist of, if it were ever truly to be experienced. Welcome back to knowingness.*

To those of you who have not skipped ahead, but are still reading this rather than the Beckett epigraph: *Well done. Now, go away and come back later, when you've been entertained, lectured, touched, shocked.*

To those of you who have returned after reading *Albert Angelo*, and are wondering whether I didn't perhaps diminish the shock by mentioning it in advance: *I apologize. That was the best I could do. Because that is the best we can do – resist the temptation to preserve ourselves from shocks, even though we often know quite a lot about them already. Avoid spoilers. Avoid creating spoilers. But I couldn't write about* Albert Angelo *without mentioning the shock. Because* Albert Angelo *turns on the shock of self-accusation.*

I have many problems with my contemporaries, but most of all with their willingness to believe they've learned from the mistakes of others – and that, as a result, they'll never make those mistakes. This, however, is knowingness rather than knowledge. Knowingness brings a suspicion of idealism. Because we have never made the mistake of having unreasonable ideals, we are comforted by knowingly calling all ideals naïve. Because this or that radicalism is said to have failed, we knowingly take it that radicalism always leads to failure.

Taking knowingness for knowledge is the worst mistake of all.

Albert Angelo is a very easy book for a certain kind of contemporary to sneer at. It is a crudely experimental novel. It is an example of a rudimentary, struggling, English postmodernism. It is, bless it, not quite clear what it wants to be.

To which I want to reply: *There is no experiment without crudity.*

Think of all modern art, from Cezanne's faulty visions of faulty vision, to the outrageous unevenness of *Les Demoiselles d'Avignon*, to Bacon's inexplicably orange *Three Studies for Figures at the Base of a Crucifixion*; from the headbanging momentum of *Boléro*, to the cut-and-pasted sound-blocks of

The Rite of Spring, to the gnarly lurches of Steve Reich's *It's Gonna Rain*; from D. H. Lawrence's bodged-together anti-psychologies, to Donald Barthelme's choreographies of elegant incoherence, to the deliberate longueurs of David Foster Wallace's *The Pale King*; from Emily Dickinson's wonky hymns to perhaps-God, to 'The Waste Land', to Sylvia Plath's brutal 'Daddy'.

These were not classical masters who had calculated the balanced effects of what they were putting in accustomed place. These were desperate strugglers with blocks and bloops of slimy, coming-alive-and-dying-and-coming-alive-again stuff.

The worst knowingness of any contemporary version of history is that it itself idealizes the way things happen. It makes masters out of strugglers. It loses a sense of events as – in their flux, in their happening – entirely unhistorical moments of snafu. It suggests a form of supreme judgment exists, if one can recognize the patterns. It has no praxis.

To which, escalating, I want to reply: *There is no experiment without uncertainty.*

When B. S. Johnson wrote *Albert Angelo*, it was an experiment in these important and easily forgotten senses: B. S. Johnson did not know that *Albert Angelo* would not be a novel that became overwhelmingly popular – a bestseller. B. S. Johnson did not know that his shocking outburst of 'OH, FUCK ALL THIS LYING!' would not become a rallying cry for all fiction. B. S. Johnson did not know that he was not fundamentally changing English writing. B. S. Johnson did not know that he was not fundamentally changing English society.

Yet which contemporary writer would think it worth writing an experimental novel in the hope of drawing attention to the government's education policy?

On the final page of the 'Disintegration' of *Albert Angelo*, B. S. Johnson's out-from-behind-the-curtain narrator writes that the book is, 'Didactic, too, social comment on teaching, to draw attention, too, to improve: but with less hope, for if the government wanted better education it could be provided easily enough, so I must conclude, again, that they specifically want the majority of children to be only partially-educated.'

B. S. Johnson had 'less hope' of this possible improvement, but he still had hope. Which contemporary writer would have any?

And finally this makes me to want to reply: *There is no experiment without hope.*

Because, *this time*, the experiment might succeed. The slimy stuff might become beautifully and permanently alive. The idealism might be fulfilled. The radicalism might generally convert. Things might change for the good, because of something written.

It would be very easy to make *Albert Angelo* seem a repository of traditional fictional pleasures. One might stoop so low as to mention Dickens. There are some fine descriptive passages, et cetera. There is even Albert's gratifyingly reactionary confession: 'Of course, I would really like to be designing a Gothic cathedral, all crockets and finials and flying buttresses,...' Which can be translated into: 'Of course, I would really like to be writing *Bleak House*, all digressions and eccentric minor characters and implied Ten Commandments,...' This reaction, however, is retracted – and the continuation applies to both Gothic cathedrals and *Bleak House*: 'but I must be of my time, ahead of my time, rather, using the materials of my time, the unacknowledged legislators, and so on, in accord with, of, my age, my time, my generation, my life.'

The greatest thing about *Albert Angelo* is its wholehearted uncertainty. Uncertainty is the substance of each passionately blocked-out sentence; uncertainty is the book's underlying oomph, push, spasm, yearn – uncertainty of its main character, an architect who does not make buildings forced to become a schoolteacher who does not want to teach and does not want to do anything but teach – uncertainty of Albert Angelo, misogynistically mourning his true love, Jenny, and their idyllic hours-among-rocks – uncertainty of B. S. Johnson speaking of himself and his art/life-struggles through Albert Angelo until he can't bear the falsity of that any longer, and then isn't sure if the attempted-truth isn't worse – uncertainty of the reader who is confronted by an anguish that mocks itself, and a laughter that wants to crawl further into the black, and a love for truth that is shockingly pure.

Toby Litt
December 2012

Publisher's Note

B. S. Johnson took an active interest in the design of his books, and the original setting of this novel has been retained.

ALBERT ANGELO

When I think, that is to say, no, let it stand, when I think of the time I've wasted with these bran-dips, beginning with Murphy, who wasn't even the first, when I had me, on the premises, within easy reach, tottering under my own skin and bones, real ones, rotting with solitude and neglect, till I doubted my own existence, and even still, today, I have no faith in it, none, so that I have to say, when I speak, Who speaks, and seek, and so on and similarly for all the other things that happen to me and for which someone must be found, for things that happen must have someone to happen to, someone must stop them. But Murphy and the others, and last but not least the two old buffers here present, could not stop them, the things that happened to me, nothing could happen to them, of the things that happened to me, and nothing else either, there is nothing else, let us be lucid for once, nothing else but what happens to me, such as speaking, and such as seeking, and which cannot happen to me, which prowl round me, like bodies in torment, the torment of no abode, no repose, no, like hyenas, screeching and laughing, no, no better, no matter, I've shut my doors against them, I'm not at home to anything, my doors are shut against them, perhaps that's how I'll find silence, and peace at last, by opening my doors and letting myself be devoured, they'll stop howling, they'll start eating, the maws now howling. Open up, open up, you'll be all right, you'll see.

from *The Unnamable*
by Samuel Beckett

for Virginia

This novel has five parts:

ONE: Prologue

Joseph said: Cocoa needs cooking in a saucepan.

  Luke said: Don't be comic.

 Albert said: They put hormones or silicones or stormcones or something in it now so's it'll mix easily in the mug.

Joseph said: Whose cocoa is it, then?

  Luke said: Why are you cooking cocoa when we haven't had any nosh anyway?

Joseph said: Sustaining, cocoa is, they give it you inside to help you suffer.

 Albert said: I'll cook while you sustain us, then. I think Graham's left some odds and ends.

Joseph said: That's it. A noshup of the lot.

  Luke said: Did you know Graham then?

 Albert said: Oh, yes, I knew Graham. Well.

Joseph said: Graham once called me a pathetic pseudo-disciple of Them.

Albert said: A double-yolker! How about that, then?

Joseph said: I thought they weren't allowed any more by the egg manufacturers?

Albert said: That's made my day! A double-yolker!

Joseph said: What happens with them? D'you get two chickens out?

Luke said: Y'know, I reckon that Graham was off his trolley. I mean, I've been here some evenings and you should have heard what was going on upstairs!

Joseph said: All through the bloody night, too.

Albert said: He was certainly unusual . . . eccentric. . . .

Luke said: Eccentric! He was bleeding round the twist, mate, straight round the twist, no doubt about that!

Joseph said: I got used to it.

Luke said: Well, I wouldn't have got used to it. Bleeding groaning and saying his prayers with beads —and the music he used to play!

Joseph said: I liked it, I liked it. I didn't understand it, but I liked it.

Albert said: Well, I shan't make a lot of noise. I like quiet. I spend a lot of time working at a drawing-board.

Luke said: You an artist, then?

Albert said: Well, sort of. I'm an architect—that is, I'm a teacher really, but I want to be an architect. No, that's the wrong way round, I'm an architect but I have to earn my living by teaching.

Joseph said: What, you do drawings of buildings and things?

Albert said: Yes.

Luke said: What buildings have you done, then?

Albert said: Ones that have actually been built?

Luke said: Yes.

Albert said: None. I just design them.

Joseph said: Sounds a bit useless to me, mate. What's the use of designing buildings if no one's going to build them?

Albert said: I do it for its own sake. You have to do something for its own sake.

Luke said: Won't anyone ever build your buildings, then?

Albert said: Oh yes, one day they'll all be built, I know.

Joseph said: When you're dead, like.

Luke said: Like poets, after they're dead.

Albert said: Like poets, just.

Luke said: Fucking lot of good that is, mate. I mean, when you're dead you're fucking dead, aren't you?

Albert said: No.

*   *   *   *   *

The first thing you see about Percy Circus is that it stands most of the way up a hill, sideways, leaning upright against the slope like a practised seaman. And then the next thing is that half of it is not there. There are trees in the circular railinged area in the middle: planes mostly, but one or two oaks and a long, hanging willow, oddly twisted like a one-legged circus tumbler. There is a little grass there, too, and rubbish of various kinds littered around—bicycle wheels, bottomless enamel buckets, tins, rotting cardboard. Some of the houses have patches where new London stocks show up yellow against the older blackened ones; then you know what happened to the rest of the Circus. New flats abut at an angle, awkwardly. A blue plaque tells you that Lenin once lived at number sixteen.

Percy Circus can be dated early Victorian by the windows, which have stucco surrounds as wide as the reveals are deep, with a scroll-bracket on either side at the top. The proportions are quite good, though the move away from Georgian is obvious except in the top and leadflashed dormers. There is stucco channelled jointing up to the bottom of the first-floor windows, which have little cast-iron balconies swelling enceintely. Each house is subtly different in its detail from each of its neighbours. The paintwork is everywhere brown and old and peeling.

Albert lived at number twenty-nine. He had one huge room on the ground floor. His drawing-board he set up overlooking the Circus, facing south, to take benefit of the light.

The previous tenant was named Graham. Joseph lived underneath, in the basement, of twenty-nine Percy Circus. Albert had a bathroom, a lavatory, and a kitchen in common with Joseph. Luke was a friend to Joseph, who happened to be visiting him at the time that the conversation already related took place. Joseph had oh many other friends, but on this particular occasion it happened to be Luke who happened to be visiting Joseph on the first evening of Albert's tenure of the room in Percy Circus. On the very special occasion of Albert's coming to number twenty-nine it happened to be Luke: Luke, to give him a name pregnant with significance.

Someone lived upstairs, above Albert. Albert did not know who lived upstairs, above him. This was enough for

Albert, to know that someone lived upstairs but not to know who it was who lived upstairs. For many it would not have been enough. They would have been out at many times, on many occasions, contriving coincidences in the hall and in the passageways and other common places, in their first week at Percy Circus. But not Albert. He heard the toings and the comings and the froings, but did not worry himself with identities. It was enough, for Albert, to know that someone lived upstairs.

TWO: Exposition

I think I shall visit my parents every Saturday, as a rule, as a habit. Occasionally Sundays: instead, though, not as well. But usually Saturdays, as a rule, as a habit almost. Yes.

I think that they are my parents, at least, yes. They have always told me that they are my parents, my father and my mother, no inconsistency on their parts. I have been fairly content to think of them as my father and my mother. Naturally, I have only their words for it. Unless you count physical resemblances. But those I have, physical resemblances, to others who do not tell me they are my father, or my mother. Not that I could not have grown like them, for I could, people do grow like other people around them, in looks, and like their animals, too: Jim Wells grew to look like a greyhound in just the couple of years he kept them. And traits, too, physical traits, and mental traits, as well, these resemble some of those of my mother and more particularly some of those of my father. But traits, traits, both physical and mental, traits one picks up from anyone. Anyone.

I shall call them my parents, in any event, it seems right to call them my parents, my mother and my father. My parents, to give them a name with which to be going on.

Every Saturday morning in the normal way I shall visit my parents. In the normal way.

They live at Hammersmith, my parents. I walk down the hill from Percy Circus, along Kings Cross Road, into Pentonville Road, towards Kings Cross. The station has two great squat stock-brick arches, their yellow uncommonly unblackened; Cubitt, the youngest, Lewis. Then there are the pseudo-Gothic excrescences of Scott's St. Pancras. I wonder shall I come to accept St. Pancras station, living so near? Or even to like it? Perhaps it is fatal to live so near to St. Pancras for an architect? Certainly it would be to bring up children here: their aesthetic would be blighted. But it seems unlikely that I shall be allowed to bring up children here.

Kings Cross is crowded, the tube station, with non-Londoners, foreigners, who do not know their ways, upfortheweekenders who stand on both sides of the escalator with too much luggage and go as far as Piccadilly.

The monotonous, regular sag and rise in the cable lines through the window opposite lulls me into drowsiness. I mean, had meant, to read. Sunlight as the train emerges before Barons Court rouses me. The first wintry unsure sunlight of spring.

This sun on St. Paul's Hammersmith lifts me. Its proportions are miraculous, miraculous. Who did it . . . Gough, yes, Gough and Roumieu, and someone else. Forget the other. My first real isometric drawing was of St. Paul's. My

first real. Miraculous. And my parents (whatever that may
mean) were married there, at St. Paul's. The flyover, Hammersmith flyover, too, pleases me. It sets off the church, is
a fine piece of architecture itself. Graceful, curving away
as though on tiptoe. But the sun emphasises which is the
better.

Under, along, down towards the river. Towards the
house of my parents.

I meet the Vicar. He looks the way he was looking before
he saw me. I look the way I was looking before I saw him.
The Christian Fellowship of Youth used to run a football
team, and we used to belong. We never used to go to
church, though. And one day he was so disgusted with us,
the Vicar, that he called us a lot of little heathens. So the
team broke away from the church and we called ourselves
Little Heathens F.C. He used to let us practise in the church
school playground, but we did not miss it much, afterwards, we used the streets instead. It was difficult though
to transfer your skills to grass, but as a result we all became
good at the unexpected-angle ball. Particularly Gerry in
goal. There was an enormous manhole cover and a kerb in
front of the yardgates we used as a goal. Gerry got so used
to expecting difficult angles at short notice that he became
one of the best goalkeepers in the junior league. Gerry
actually went on and played regularly in the Combination
side for Fulham. I had a trial for Chelsea myself, when I
was about sixteen, up near the Welsh Harp at Hendon it
was, their trial ground. But I had a wet dream the night
before because I had been saving up for a week before-
hand, and I played far below my best. Not that I really
think that I would have made the pro game anyway: no
concentration if I was not completely interested. Start of
a season, I would play well because I was interested,

because I cared. Then after a few games my interest would go, though I still wanted to play well, and my game would go right off. Used to play left-half or left-back. Worked out a great understanding with Stan, our left-winger. He was as fast as a whippet. He could do the hundred yards in evens without really trying. Stan still lives near and has a fat wife and two whippety kids. I still see him sometimes, but hardly ever to speak to. The Vicar I see even less often. He looks the way he was looking before he saw me. I look the way I was looking before I saw him.

They rent it, my parents, the house, squarish 1880-looking, so undistinguished that I have never bothered to find out who built it and exactly when. Undistinguished, that is, except for the comic portico over the door: nine steps leading up to it, two plain columns with cushion capitals and a severely-moulded entablature. The grey stucco is cracked off in some places, but painted over regardless by my father. But this portico I am very fond of since I used to use it as a permanent set in my film day-dreams and acts: I would make exits and entrances and imagine a vast audience watching every movement I made. This behaving as though an audience were watching has become part of me, is my character, is me, and on one level I am always thinking and acting in a film for such a film audience.

In this house, in my parents' house, my parents' home, all affection is channelled through the dog. No one is affectionate to anyone else except through the dog. I make a fuss of the dog. Fortunately he is a sensible and a lovable dog.

I accept a mug of instant coffee from my mother.

"It's made with all milk," she says, my mother, and she is proud.

All milk, I query literally in my mind, all *milk*, and remember the war. She has a new hat, and puts it on to show me. Then she comes to asking me what she had wanted to blurt out as soon as she saw me.

"And how are you looking after yourself in your new flat?"

I answer formally. She seems reassured, perhaps unwillingly.

"Have you got another school yet?"

I point out to her that the holidays are still on, and that they therefore do not know what vacancies there will be for supply teachers.

"Why don't you take a permanent job, Albert? You've been doing this supply now for three years. You're twenty-eight, now, you know."

I know that very well, today, though there are days when I know it far less well. I answer her question as I have answered it many times before: I am an architect, not a teacher, and I will not tie myself to a term's notice even though it does mean the insecurity and constant changing of schools involved in supply work. She does not understand. She did not understand before. She has never understood. I do not mind that she does not understand, now, now I do not care that she does not understand. There was a time when I was concerned that she should understand.

I ask her where my father is.

"On the dyke."

I wander out into the little garden. My father comes out, clipping together the two halves of his Boy Scout belt. He wears braces as well, my father, not exactly a pessimist, but always prepared.

"Wotcher, mate," he says, my father, and he grins.

One of the few warm things I remember about the war was my father calling me 'mate' in his letters home.

I play cricket with my father, in the little garden. We use a watering-can, a broom, and a practice golfball he found down along the towpath. I give him first innings and cannot get him out. Eventually he gives me an easy catch. Then he has me out third ball. He uses his off-spinner. Incredible, it is, his golfball offspinner, but I should know it by now. He pretends he did not see it beat me or hear the hollow clunk on the can. I draw his attention to both. He is still batting when my mother comes out to call us in to lunch.

My father liked my mother because she turned up for their first assignation even though it was raining. Here was reliability. And fortitude.

For lunch we have beef. I enjoy lunch. I offer the dog a piece of gristly beef for which I have no use.

"You'll make him sick," says my mother.

"You'll make him constipated," says my father.

The dog accepts my offer, swallows it without chewing, and sits back confused about whether sickness or constipation is now expected of him.

I go to football with my father in the afternoon, after my mother has fed us, has fulfilled her function, has performed her duty, as she sees it, as mothers see it. I catch a number eleven bus with my father as far as Fulham Broadway. Walham Green it used to be called, when I first came here, and when my father first came here, too, I suppose, that long ago. I and my father join thousands of others jostling along Fulham Road at a pointlessly fast pace. My father buys two programmes. I pay for us both at the turnstiles.

First I and then my father climb the steep concrete steps

behind the main terrace. I note again the *ad hoc*, piecemeal construction of the terrace: a huge earth mound formed from the excavated centre with a steeply cantilevered shell on it. Badly finished, shuttering marks: not that such marks are not of the nature of the material, of the nature of concrete, for they are, but they can be well left or ill left. Here they are ill left.

Chelsea's play is intensely aggravating, by turns appallingly bad and supremely skilful. They always play like this. Chelsea supporters are men of a special cast of mind, and widely cosmopolitan: all they have in common is this need to become emotionally involved with a team which can play as well as any and worse than any. Men who need to experience a wildly fluctuating range of emotions within ninety minutes. They would not come to Stamford Bridge if the team played any differently. Whoever manages the team, whoever plays in the team, the tradition is the same, is perpetuated.

I remember, in swearing, shouting, and roaring with the rest, today, the first time I heard my father swear, at a football match, how somehow it made us closer, me having heard him swear, as though against the women, the two of us, closer.

In the interval it is cold. I feel the cold, my father feels the cold. I can see my father feels the cold badly. I promise to buy him a season ticket for a seat in the stand when I get my first big commission. He does not answer. I know that he regards this as about as likely as him winning the pools. He gives me an apple, and polishes one for himself against the lapel of his old raincoat.

The second half begins. And ends. Chelsea lose three–two after leading two–nil at one point. Satisfied with our dissatisfaction, I and my father and the crowd squirm away from Stamford Bridge. I blame myself for the defeat, since I lost interest ten minutes after half-time, stopped willing them to win. I had been trying to find an original solution for a stadium to hold a hundred thousand which did not crib from Nervi.

A bus is not caught by either my father or myself, a number eleven, that is, the one we came by, on our return. We walk down the whole length of North End Road. We always do this. We enjoy the street market. Occasionally my father buys something. Usually it is vegetables. Today he buys some Felixmeat for the dog. The dog is a perverse dog. Felixmeat is his delight, nothing can make earth seem more like heaven than Felixmeat, in his view. I feel it is fortunate that not more of us have views like this.

I catch with my father a number twenty-seven bus several minutes after arriving at the bus-stop in Hammersmith Road at the end of North End Road. The northern end of North End Road, that is. We could have caught a number nine or a number seventy-three, to place them in numerical order, had either of these splendid numbers been opportune. But we catch a number twenty-seven back to Hammersmith, my father, and I. The numbers are related: the square root of nine, three, multiplied by nine gives you twenty-seven; and seven added to three brings you back to nine again, if you take one off. Furthermore, there is a three in seventy-three. The numbers of these three (*again!*) buses running along the Hammersmith Road are not related by accident, these things are no coincidences. Anyone who thinks they are accidents or coincidences probably does not believe in parthogenesis either. To say nothing of god. But no one ever says nothing of god. I feel that this may well be a large part of the trouble.

My father talks to me on the twenty-seven.

"Have you been to see about teaching up at the Angel?"

I tell him almost exactly what I told my mother earlier.

"It's a tough area, mate, I shouldn't think they get many teachers to stay. The kids are very tough."

I tell him that I think he must be exaggerating, and that the children I have been teaching in West London have not been easy to control. I feel fairly confident about taking any class after the variety of three years' supply.

"It's really your mother who worries about you not having a job."

I tell him I have a job: I am an architect.

My mother has a special tea ready. I can see my father is very glad to be indoors out of the cold.

"Taters," he says. "Taters in the mould."

But there are kippers and hot rolls and English butter and fancy cream cakes. She is being good to me, my mother. I do not know whether it is because she wants to make me welcome after missing me or because she wants to make me regret leaving home.

When Jenny left me, betrayed me for a cripple whom she imagined to need her more, my mother said never mind, perhaps he would die and then I could have her back again.

* * * * *

You have a phone call from them sometimes, but usually you have to go to the office and wait until someone wants **you.**

You have a phone call from them this first morning. The woman at the office gives you directions to the school, and you look it up in your *A to Z* to make quite sure. You put in a briefcase those textbooks experience has suggested will cover most of the subjects you are likely to be required to teach.

You walk out of Percy Circus down past the doctor's surgery. Vernon Baptist Church, rosebushbeds, the public patch with the public seats, traffic, traffic, at the one-way system intersection, across Kings Cross Road, the Hansler Arms, Grove Fisheries, Connaught Dairy, Express Dining Rooms, the Northumberland Arms, the sun on Cobden Buildings with their curious half-exposed central stairway and castiron ornament, *Sausage Cases* (The Oppenheimer Casing Co. (U.K.) Ltd.), Caxton Printing Co. (Kings Cross) Ltd., The Susan Lawrence Hostel, the back of the Welsh Chapel, Ladies, Gentlemen, Radios, Launderette, Suits. . . .

You catch a number 214 bus outside Henekey's, past St. James's, which reminds you of Adam, but you realise that he can hardly have had anything to do with it, to the top of Pentonville Road. The end of a Georgian terrace against the skyline, stacks and terracotta, graceful, peaceful, very right. Flowers on a surprising bank to the right, a grass mound with shrubs, flowering yellow and leaved laurel-green, walled with broken glass and coiled barbed wire on top; you wonder what it is. It is in the centre of a square with tall late Georgian second-ratings with mansard roofs: the pitch of the mansards is particularly well-chosen, subtle. It pleases you. Claremont Square, it was, you notice, as the bus passes the farther side. You will walk that way, you decide, soon.

Angel Mews, another garden. Colebrooke Row, lovely,

backs of fourth-ratings, all pleases you this morning by its grace and proportion, in the sunlight, down the City Road, to City Road Basin, the bus takes you, you leave the bus, you walk through sidestreets for nearly ten minutes before you find the school.

You open a blackiron door into the playground, and go down a flight of steps. The wall you have just come through forms one side; the school forms another; and tall factory buildings, with heavy wire shields over their windows, complete the other two sides of the playground's quadrilateral. At this level the building is partly open, supported on great blackened stockbrick piers, and providing dark shelter. Down the centre runs a fletton wall broken in its length only by a door, later than the rest of the building but well on its way to becoming as blackened, dividing the sexes. Against opposite walls, projecting little more than three feet, are identically-built lavatories, a postern for each sex. They look like air-raid shelter entrances, narrow, claustrophobic. The asphalt surface of the playground has a very noticeable slope.

You see a girl of about nine come out from a postern, still hitching herself comfortable, and you ask her to take you to the Headmaster.

The Headmaster is formal, apart, preoccupied. He introduces you to his Deputy Head, Mr. Coulter. Mr. Coulter does not like you. He does not like any supply teacher. Supply teachers mean inconvenience to him. They upset his timetable and they are often untrained and incompetent.

As he takes you along square stonefloored tunnels to your classroom he expresses his dislike, oh so politely, by finding out why you are not in a permanent teaching post when he hears that you are trained and qualified.

"Ah, an architect *manqué*," he smiles unpleasurably,

opening a classroom door and requiring almost imperatively that you enter first.

The class is relatively quiet. Mr. Coulter calls them to attention.

"Thank you, 3B, for helping us by behaving yourselves while left alone. I shall see that you gain five Merit Points for it. Now, as you know, Mr. MacKenzie is away ill, and Mr. . . . what is your name?"

You tell him, although the Headmaster had told him when he introduced you.

". . . and Mr. Albert is going to take you until Mr. MacKenzie is quite well again. I'm sure that you will do everything you can to help Mr. Albert while he is here. If anyone does misbehave, then Mr. Albert will tell me, won't you, Mr. Albert—and you know what that means, don't you? Christopher Arbor does, don't you, Christopher? You ask Christopher what happens to those who make a nuisance of themselves!"

He turns to you.

"I don't think you'll have much trouble with them, Albert," he says in a lowered voice. "MacKenzie keeps them very much under his thumb. Now the register and dinner money haven't been done. I'll lend you my red pen, if you'll be a good man and be sure to let me have it back at playtime."

You have a red pen. They love you to have your own red pen.

"Oh. Well, in that case I'll leave you to it, to sink or swim. If you need me, my classroom is one floor up, at the end of the corridor right above the one we came along. Fit, then?"

You smile your fitness to teach 3B. He goes to the door, and then remembers something.

"Oh, MacKenzie does dinner duty on Mondays, when he's here, that is, Albert. I trust you have no objections to dinner duty?"

Yes, you have. But you always do it just the same.

"Ah, Albert," he says, "you're too young to have been a teacher before the war. Then we had to bring our own food and cook it in the staffroom. Or go out to dinner, which few of us could afford. Now there's none of that. And the children then often didn't see a square meal from one week's end to the next."

You are not objecting to there being school dinners. You were a child at a London school yourself just before the war. You think the scheme is admirable. But it should be run by non-teaching staff.

"Well, the union has been advocating that for many years now, Albert, many years," Mr. Coulter says.

You restrain your contempt for the union with difficulty.

"It'll come, Albert, it'll come," he says. "Meanwhile— one floor up, at the end of the corridor right above the one we came along."

You are glad he is gone. You smile and look at the class.

"Right, 3B," you say, "just until I get used to things, I'd like you to read quietly to yourselves. You all have your own reading books, don't you?"

Brightly yes.

"Until playtime, then, read. Or look at the pictures if reading is not your best subject. When is playtime, by the way? Christopher Arbor?"

Give him responsibility; he should be on your side if he is a troublemaker. Perhaps in a sense prove Coulter wrong, too.

"Five past eleven, sir," a boy says. � Potato face, potential boxer's, wide eyes, retroussé nose, wellblack hair, blue pullover. ↳

"Thanks, Chris," you say. He looks pleased at attention being paid to him that is not threatening; or perhaps he thinks he has found a soft teacher.

You sit down. You are glad to sit down. You open the single central drawer of the scored and inkstained desk. Under the register and the dinner book is a litter of school-children's valuables: marbles, sweets, plastic whistles, a spring balance, razorblades, three thimbles, handkerchiefs, keys, chewed rubbers, brushes, pens, pencils, useless plastic parts, ballpen refills, cereal manufacturers' lures, a Durex packet, and a long blunt sheathknife.

You open the register, and glance down the names. Several Greek-looking ones, a Mustapha, and half a dozen Irish. Not a West Indian district, apparently. You look for special notes: there is only one, Linda Taylor, mild epileptic, besides three with 'S' against their names for spectacles. You look round, and see that only two children are wearing glasses: both are boys, and looking again at the names see the third to be a girl. You decide to demonstrate that you have knowledge of them, and there-fore a certain mysterious professional power over them.

"Gloria Canning: why aren't you wearing your glasses this morning?" you demand.

"Please, sir, I left them at home. My mum forgot to remind me." ⌐Small, dark, ovoid face, squareset eyes, block chin, homepermed hair, whitelace blouse.⌐

"Please don't forget tomorrow, then. And you're old enough now not to need your mother to remind you."

3B. Third year, second stream, nine-to-ten-year-olds. How many streams in this school? Difficult to tell how many. 3B will not be the brightest, anyway. Taking J.L.E. next January. Only another nine months, so you should do a fair proportion of formal work with them.

Oversquare room with high, pocked ceiling. White-flaking decoration. Brown up to dado, a green line, then chalky green to ceiling. Woodblock floor treated shinily to prevent splinters. Furniture old, apart from new pair of cupboards. White sashes, three large lights on one side. Reproduction on opposite wall of winsome girl, red-cheeked at embroidery. Vertical sliding blackboards, worn, messy. Boardrubber bald.

"You two, stop talking! You were told to read. What're your names? And stand up!"

You must always start harder than you intend to go on: never the other way round.

"Please, sir, they don't know what you say to them."

"They're Cypriots, sir."

"They can't understand, sir."

"Oh. Thank you."

⤳Dark hair, olive faces, rounded, a little simian, beautifully-shaped heads, remarkably alike.

"How many of the others do not understand English?"

Four.

Give them games to play with in the formal lessons, books to look at, and personal coaching, ha, and try to give as many other lessons as possible that do not involve reading or writing without depriving the other children. Like painting. Yes, you can give a painting lesson after play.

"Now, will you all please answer your names as I call them. Rita Allen."

"Yes, sir."

"Hilary Bullivant."

"Yes, sir."

"Jaclynne Caylor."

"Here, sir."

"Gloria Canning."

"Here."

"Sherry Clift."

"Yes, sir."

"Janet Collings."

"Present."

"Anne Foley."

"Here."

"Nevin Georgiou."

"Yes."

She knows one word of
English, at least.

"Doreen Langley."

"Yes, sir."

"Ann Liddiard."

"Present, sir."

"Denise Murphy."

"Yes, sir."

"Felicity Murphy."

"Yes, sir."

"Are you two cousins? No? Related in any way?"

"No, sir."

"Oh. Kate O'Reilly. Kate O'Reilly?"

"Absent, sir."

"Sir, I saw her up Old Street yesterday, with her mum."

"Do you know why she isn't here?"

"No, sir."

"Then there wasn't much point in telling me you saw
her up Old Street yesterday with her mum, then, was
there? Stella Riordan."

"Here, sir."

"Gladys Saintly."

"Present."

"Linda Salter."

"Yes, sir."

"Sonia Smith."

"Here, sir."

"Georgina Stoneham."

"Here, sir."

"Yvonne Stonehouse."

"Here, sir."

"Linda Taylor. Linda Taylor? Anyone know why Linda's away?"

"Please, sir, she's got fits."

"She had one in class, sir."

"She bit Mr. MacKenzie, sir."

"That's enough! Brenda Trussell."

"Yes, sir."

"Elaine Vaughan."

"Yes, sir."

"Lynn Waters."

"Yes."

"Now the boys. Christopher Arbor."

"Yerp!"

> *You look hard at him. You decide to let him get away with it this time.*

"David Bufton."

"Yerp. Sir."

"Alan Burdick."

"Yer-r-r-r-r-p!"

"Look, the next boy who tries to be funny while I'm calling the register is going to regret it. Georgiou Constantenou."

"Yes, sir."

"James Day. James Day?"

> *You will risk a joke.*

"James Day seems away."

        Good, they laughed a little.

"Owen Evans."

"Here, sir."

"George Ellett."

"Here, sir."

"John Hammett."

"Yes, sir."

"Barry Hilton."

"Present, sir."

"Roger Lord."

"Present."

"Eray Mustapha."

"Yes, sir."

"Eray? Which one's Eray? Can you understand any more English, Eray?"

"Yes, sir."

        Accent like any other North Londoner's. Must have been born here.

"Good. John Nash."

        John Nash and Regent Street and the Quadrant and All Souls' and the Prince Regent and the Haymarket Theatre and bits of Buckingham Palace, you think, John Nash.

"Yes, sir."

"Andreas Neo . . . Neophytos."

"Yes, sir."

"Derek Pearce."

"Present."

"Alan Pearson."

"Present. Sir."

"William Rollings. William Rollings. Away?"

"Yes, sir."

"Away, sir."

"Fedros Stavrikes."

"Yes, sir."

"Daniel Williams."

"Here, sir."

"James Wilson."

"Yes, sir."

"Right. Thank you."

Twenty-one girls here. Seventeen boys.

"Now I want all those who are staying to lunch, dinner, that is, today, to bring out their money when I call their names."

This takes you until nearly playtime. You fail to avoid awkwardness, embarrassment, shame, over those who do not bring money out but have free dinners. Not for the first time.

At eleven you remember to direct that the milk be given out. At playtime you dismiss them and Christopher Arbor shows you the way to the staffroom.

You face the staff, an outsider. No one talks to you except Mr. Coulter, briefly, and an old woman of about thirty, at length. She talks sweetly to you, who would rather be left alone, the professional supply. Through your talking you listen to the rest of the staff. The men are noisily discussing their combined perm entry which narrowly failed to win the week before. The women are shy, the other unmarried ones, and the married ones are aggressive and make loud remarks about the Headmaster's laziness and criminal unfitness.

You are given a cup of tea, and charged twopence for it.

Always in supply there is this mysterious figure whom you are replacing. You try to build up your own conception of him from what the others let fall in conversation, from his room, his desk, his children. Mr. MacKenzie. Whom you are replacing.

Your painting lesson goes well, though there is a lot of noise. You pin a piece of sugarpaper to the board and show them the elements of a simple landscape. On the top three-fifths of the paper you lay a greyblue wash, and on the bottom two-fifths an earthbrown one. You run some black mountains across the division. The children murmur then as they see, as the mountains make the picture stand out, become real to them. You are pleased at their re-action. You add a full moon, and then tell them that once they have reached this stage themselves then they may put whatever they wish in the foreground.

You walk around, watching them working. Some start with the moon. You try to remain patient, kind. It begins to be a strain. You go back for relief to your own painting, and quickly rough in a Doric portico flanked by colon-nades. You enjoy it. You hear some giggling going on, and turn. A group of boys. They quickly split up, and one tries to hide a painting as they see you noticing. You walk slowly up and demand the painting. In the foreground are hardly identifiable animals with television aerials on their heads, yoked to a sleigh. Underneath each is a series of brown splodges, and, leaving no room for dubiety as to what was represented, an arrow and the word *shit*. You conceal your amusement with difficulty, confiscate the drawing for your collection, and stand the boys out in the front facing the board.

Mr. Coulter comes to fetch you just before the bell for

lunch. The children are still painting. You tell them to clear up now. They do so readily: you are not sure whether it is because you have control over them or because Mr. Coulter is there. You cover up the painting of the incontinent animals with the register as Mr. Coulter moves towards your desk.

Mr. Coulter takes you down to the dining-hall. Long rows of cream Formica-topped skeletal tables, skeletal chairs with steam-moulded laminated wooden seats and backs, lines of children at two closed hatches. The noise is tremendous, due largely to the acoustic properties of the hall. Mr. Coulter goes to the dais, picks up a large brass handbell and rings it violently. Most of the children stop talking.

"*When* you stop chattering, *then* you can have your dinners!" he bellows. He picks on a child at random. "Gerald Thompson, you can't stop talking so you'll have to wait until the end. Go to the very back of the queue. Go on, *move*, boy! Anyone else?"

They are silent now.

"Mrs. Goodman, I think we are just about ready to start dinner now."

The hatches open, and in a remarkably short time the lines have disappeared and the tables have filled with small children, eating and talking. The noise is worse than before, there now being added the clatter of knives and forks. Mr. Coulter tells you to go around giving permission to those who have finished and are sitting up straight with their arms folded to take their plates out and collect their puddings.

The tablemanners are appalling by Mr. Coulter's standards. You notice him correcting one eight-year-old girl for some time. You do not attempt to do anything similar yourself: these children and their manners are the product of their environment, and therefore suit that environment. You are not sure enough of your own standards to take the responsibility of imposing them on these children for whom they would probably be quite inappropriate.

You do, however, very surely deal with two boys who are delightedly spattering each other with mashed potato.

School dinner is finished in just over fifteen minutes, the slower eaters being chivvied and forced. Mr. Coulter tells you how they pride themselves on this speed.

"So even if you do consider it an imposition, Albert," he says as you climb back towards the staffroom and your own meal, "you can see that at this school we make dinner duty as painless as possible."

The staffroom is on the top floor. There is a view from it out to the south-east, over the city. You are grateful for it. Some of the tower blocks are very good in their own right, though too many of them have services untidily designed on their roofs. After lunch you sit sketching it in your notebook, the skyline: blocks, spires, St. Paul's. The blocks set off the cathedral: none are as tall: their rectangularity against the dome's sweet curve.

The rest of the staff chattter and laugh: the air becomes polluted with the smoke of their camaraderie. They think you are unsociable. Even the woman of thirty does not talk to you after she has given you another cup of tea and charged you another twopence for it. You do not mind.

You teach them simple sentence construction during the first session of the afternoon.

You read them a story during the second session of the afternoon.

You feel exhausted at the end of the afternoon.

You decide to walk home slowly, up the City Road,

towards the Angel. City Arms; St. Mark's Hospital for Fistula &c.; Mona Lisa Cafe Restaurant; vast anonymous factory block shouldering Georgian first-ratings mainly used for light industries; Albion House with two lovely bow-fronts spoilt by nursery stickers inside the windows and two comically sentimental plaster dogs guarding the steps.

Sale Closing Down. Aspenville wallpaper. Claremont Mission. Overgrown gardens this side. Claremont Square. The bank again, yellow, saffron, green. Across Amwell Street, down Great Percy Street, to the Circus.

You feel far less tired when you reach your flat.

You walk to school as well the next morning, for your second day at St. Sepulchre's. You look forward to teaching. You think of it as a great privilege, to be allowed to work amongst children. Very worthwhile, very satisfying. You think of these as commonplaces, but true and relevant, and remember that this is how you always feel, enthusiastic and dedicated, at the start of a term. Then disenchantment sets in, after perhaps two weeks.

But this second morning you look forward to teaching. You arrive early. You talk with the early children as friends, interesting yourself in their interests. When the class has assembled you say good morning to them, smiling, and they respond readily.

You try the standard jokes:

"All those who are absent please put up their hands."

They are allowed to laugh at this.

And, later:

"Now who's going to have super delicious school dinners?"

They are allowed to groan at this, in a derisive manner.

You like your class. You want to teach them well, as a result. Mr. Coulter interrupts your first lesson, ostensibly to tell you that you are on playground duty today, but really, you are sure, to check up on you. The class is working quietly, and you are giving personal attention to one child when he comes in. You are pleased he has not caught you out. He tells you that no ballgames are allowed in the playground because children have too frequently been knocked over and injured whilst playing them.

When you see them in the confined area of the playground, you can understand why. But, deprived of ballgames, the boys have evolved other ways of playing. The playground has a slope of perhaps one in twelve in its fifteen-yard length, and groups of boys link arms against the factory wall at the back and rush down it. Anyone in their way is knocked down. This game they call Chariots. You stop them, feeling a spoilsport as you do so. Even so, you notice that at any given moment there seem to be just as many boys on the ground, fighting, or being tripped, or falling.

You go through the door in the fletton wall to the girls' side. You notice that the wall is badly laid. You presume that this was once one playground, and that, divided, it now serves for more children.

Many of the girls are standing in small groups, talking. Others chase round these groups. Some of those from your class run over to you and cling to your arms looking up at you and smiling and laughing. You are pleased with their attention, but quite relieved at the same time that no adult can see you; especially no adult who knows you.

⌐Dark, red cheeks, dirty mouth.⌐   ⌐So fair, skin pale as white vitriolite, one incisor broken at the corner.⌐ ⌐Strong, neat, curiously twisted smile.⌐   ⌐Tall, shy, never taking her eyes from you. ⌐

You shiver slightly; you wish you had put on your

overcoat. You wonder how the wind penetrates such an enclosed space.

You wonder why there is no woman teacher on duty in this playground.

⤳ Jenny! Just like Jenny. Not in your class. That square set of the shoulders, the same type of face, but coarser, oh, far coarser than Jenny's. But eyes just as lovely, just as treacherous. ⤳

A boy comes running through the door up to you and says that someone is hurt. Gently, you make the girls leave hold of you and go through to see. A boy has grazed his hand against the wall. You ask who attends to such things in this school, and then send the boy with two of his friends to the school secretary.

You see by your watch that playtime has ended, but you give them three minutes more before blowing your whistle. They line up reasonably quickly, and do not talk. You are surprised. You stand in the doorway attempting to control the files in both playgrounds at once.

The first period after lunch you feel relaxed, completely in control of your class. You begin a geography lesson which turns into a lesson on London then into a lesson on architecture. You try very hard to make it interesting and understandable to your children. That they are quiet seems to indicate that you are succeeding: there is only one slight disturbance when Bufton, toying with a pencil, sends it skittering across the classroom; and this you deal with patiently. Even the Greek Cypriots seem to be watching and listening, though presumably they can understand very little of what you are saying. The bell cuts short your lesson while they are still attentive and not restive.

Before going down to the playground you ask Mr. Coulter what special arrangements there are for teaching the Cypriots. He is non-committal about it, resents your asking the question, and implies that it is not really the concern of a supply teacher.

⌐Face of a failed saint, boyblue eyes, hair like a drummer's brush.⌐   ⌐Ochre smudge of a face, narrow eyes, soft black hair, lace collar and white press-stud shoes. ⌐

"'Ere, sir, d'you know some boy, 'e said there was a pole frough the norf and souf poles!"

Your arms ache where they drag on you.

You set the rest of your class to read, and have the Cypriots out as a group. Eray Mustapha, whom you had hoped to use as an interpreter, you find speaks Turkish and can no more communicate with the Greeks than you can. You take a simple reading book with large coloured pictures in it, and, from a slight knowledge of classical Greek, you identify such objects and ideas as you can for them: φίλος, χωρα, μουσα, νησος, λεω, λογος, πολί, ἐρως, πατερ, γενες.

Fedros and particularly Andreas are quick to pick up the words, and point to other objects and give them their Greek names in return for your giving their English ones; but the girl Nevin is shy, and you have great difficulty in persuading her to join in.

At the end of the afternoon you feel very tired. You have tripled your Greek vocabulary. You catch a bus home.

The next day it is raining. On going into your class you find a stranger there. You assume he is Mr. MacKenzie, though he does not introduce himself. He does not seem curious about the work you have been doing with his class. Mr. Coulter comes in to tell you that they have phoned from the office to tell you to go on to Wormwood Street Junior Boys' School. Mr. Coulter does not say goodbye to you, and you are overpolite to him. On your way out you see some more of your class, and you smile at them but do not stop to talk.

In your *A to Z* you find that Wormwood Street is in the City, just to the south of Liverpool Street Station. You catch a bus to Finsbury Circus and walk through crowds of crowdressed men and artificially coloured officebirds. It pleases you to walk slowly, to be going about something so totally different from these people.

The school does not look like a school; it is scarcely distinguishable from the commercial buildings around it. Inside, you can hear a hymn being sung somewhere on the floors above, and an odd slishing sound of traffic on the wet road outside.

The school secretary seats you in the Headmaster's room until assembly is over. He is a round, meaty man, the Headmaster, when he comes. The school is a small one, and you are to take the single first-year class in place of a teacher who has been released for two days to attend a course.

All boys. Superbly natural haircuts. Real. ⌐ Perpetually grinning eyes, skijump nose, thin lips.↲ ⌐Blacker than you would think possible, starred by teeth white as the weathered western face of Portland stone, eyes brown as brazil nuts.↲ ⌐Blue eyes, staring, postbox mouth, ears like open cardoors. ↲

A new desk, hardly kicked. A worn dirty cushion upon which you feel unable to bring yourself to sit. Grey cupboards, pitted blackboard, no decoration at all on the walls except for a frayed canvas map of the world as Mercator projected it. A lean budgerigar in a rusting cage making untimely interruptions.

The modern method: tables grouped in threes, so that some children have to turn their heads to face you. Should be grouped according to relative intelligence. You look round to try to see which is which. There is an art which can tell something of the mind's construction in the face.

You set them to read, to start with, the opening gambit, unchanging. They are used to having a woman teacher, but they are not well disciplined. They begin to get on top of you. You must clamp down on them. You hit one of them. It is the wrong one to hit: he has a bad ear, the others tell you, in chorus, and you have hit it. He stares through the window to hide his tears from you, infinitely pathetic, for the rest of the lesson. You feel guilty, but suppress the feeling. It is an enormous effort. You worry about the boy, quietly, for the rest of the morning.

You use eccentrically coloured chalks, for relief.

At lunchtime you do not stay in the staffroom after you have eaten. You go back to your classroom and teach obscenities to the budgie. He does not learn: either.

At the end of the day you are depressed. It is at such times that you feel the loss of Jenny most. Somehow, she represents the depression, is responsible for it in a basic but indirect way; but responsible in a way that you admit is not her fault. Paradox. At such times she should be here to solace you.

You walk home despondently.

The second day at Wormwood is worse. You despair of being able to teach. Even when you try to entertain you evoke little response from the boys. Yet you like them. You hate yourself. By midday the strain of being responsible for every child whose nose is bleeding is almost at breaking-point.

You are very glad and very tired when the end of the day comes and you leave Wormwood.

They send you the next day, on the Friday, the last day of the first week, to Crane Grove Secondary, up past

Highbury Corner, off the Holloway Road. The five- and six-storey schools in this part stand above the three-storey streets like chaotic castellations. Dead cinemas and a musichall sadden corners, abandoned. Only Arsenal Stadium, older-looking in its outdated modernity than last century's houses, competes in height with the dark red brick, stonedressed schools. Swart sleek diesels shaped as functionally as otters pass and re-pass solemnly between strips of houses at eaves-level pulling trains of rust-stained wagons.

You spend all day teaching simple English to the third-year classes, fourteen-year-olds who have very little interest in learning: they are waiting only to leave school. You try to arouse their interest by pointing out how basic a knowledge of at least English must be. One boy says he can read the racing, and that that's enough for him.

⌐A mulatta, next to him, with negroid features, coffee-coloured, frizzy hair tending towards fairness.⌐

They sit, large and awkward at the aluminium-framed tables and chairs, men and women, physically, whom you are for today trying to help to teach to take places in a society you do not believe in, in which their values already prevail rather than yours. Most will be wives and husbands, some will be whores and ponces: it's all the same; any who think will be unhappy, all who don't think will die.

Even the lavatory-gothic of the Union Chapel in Compton Terrace cannot make you smile on your way back home, nor the glimpse of Barry's Holy Trinity in Cloudesley Square encourage you by a reminder that a good architect's early work may be poor.

The end of the last day of the first week.

* * * * *

He must have seen her on the first day at college, but the earliest clear recollection that he had was of noticing as she passed in the corridor, once, the just too large and hooked nose, her only fault. He was pleased about this fault: for otherwise she was so very fine, a woman of nineteen, holding herself very squarely, with wide shoulders, long arms and legs which tapered subtly and gracefully, and breasts to just the right proportion. Dark-haired, she seemed proud, haughty, and unattainable to him at first, and he hated her for being these to him, and was glad about her nose.

She thought him arrogant, and sensed that he felt himself superior to the rest of their year. She noticed his neat suits, and that he always wore white shirts with stiff collars and unpatterned ties. This formality in his dress was counterpointed by an intellectual eccentricity which at first she resented, then admired, and finally came almost to worship. She found herself taking his side in defending the indefensible propositions and situations into which his originality of thought had taken him. And physically she felt he was her equal, right for her, big, hard, everything physically about him was big and hard.

It grew between, love, of a kind, love, more in him than in her, but love, a good love, of its kind.

He felt it as a desire to absorb her yet to become lost in her, for as long as he could see, for as long as he could feel, to merge with her, completely, utterly, achieve the completion of his self in her.

She felt it as a triumph for her self, that she could win him, as she had recently failed to win a lover host to an incurable crippling disease, as a temporary and transitional absorption in which she could destroy the image of this former love.

It was created, fostered, nurtured, cultured, maintained by the situation, this love, by the being together within college, each day. For him, it had as great an existence outside, too; for her, it had a place, but a small place, in the background when she was at home with her parents.

He was used by it; she used it; it, this love between.

He had talked with her about architecture, had given some of his enthusiasm for it to her, and had one day invited her to a lecture on modern architecture at the I.C.A. The first time alone together, he and she, having always before been in the company of other people at college. He was nervous, and talked too much and too quickly. She listened, too conscious of wanting to hear, and tried to make him feel easier.

But by the end of the evening it was warm and good between them.

He walked with her, she walked with him, along Piccadilly, down Lower Regent Street, through the Palladian-Greek vista formed by Smirke's Royal College of Physicians, Wilkins' National Gallery, and Gibbs' St. Martin's-in-the-Fields. Then he showed her Hungerford Lane, under the rsjs, past the doorways of arch-lockups, the several smells of various different storages, and the roofline through the gap up to the right like a random clerestory mullioned by fire escapes and black leaning stacks: and where he would have kissed her, there in the winedark shadows beneath the groined arches before they turned out through the garage into Villiers Street, but for his need to do so anti-romantically, to prove it, the romance, the love. So he waited until they were in the well-lit vaulted approaches to the footpath of Hungerford Bridge, and then in the middle of a sentence he stopped and turned her towards him, and she was waiting for him and ready and he kissed her and then moved his head to kiss her neck and she put down her handbag and held him to her and he kissed her fully and felt her lips grow warm and knew and gently used his tongue as he ended the kiss to tell her more of him and when she felt him leave go of her she felt she knew his body already, hard and solid, big and hard, and he felt he knew her body already, as well, warm and pliant, smooth and warm.

And he and she had linked arms tightly and naturally and walked off across the Bridge in step, his body and her body complementary, to Waterloo where she was to catch a train to her home in Sutton.

He made her miss one train to catch a later one; then she made him wait for her while she missed the next one; and finally she caught her last train that night; he saw her on to her last train that night.

"There will be other times," she said, Jenny.

"All the other times in the world," he said, Albert.

* * * * *

We see much more of each other now: at about the same time as I moved up to the Angel, Terry's wife Janine left him and he came back to live with his parents in Clerkenwell.

We have an odd sort of reluctant friendship in which each of us depends on the other for things the other does not really know he is giving. Physically, we are very disparate, but we think the same way about many things: and we were both London kids.

We go out fairly late: after nine, say, and have a few drinks, and then after they close we go searching for various places which stay open all night.

Most usually we head down City Road, then sharp left at Old Street Station, bear right into Great Eastern Street and Commercial Street, down to Whitechapel. Sometimes we stop there at Aldgate for cockles or prawns at Tubby Isaacs', but more often we will go straight on down to Cable Street, and Terry will park this Fiat he runs in Wellclose Square.

Visually, architecturally, Cable Street, Cablestrasse, The Strasse, at night excites us: everywhere we go in this part of Stepney there are Georgian façades in all stages of repair, from the one beautifully-kept house in Wellclose Square to others with skeletal dormers from which the lead and boards have been stripped. There are bomb-derelict warehouses, too, one with a thick first-storey drawbridge suspended from chains above a gulf.

But we really come down Cable Street because of the allnight cafés, because there we can always be sure of something going on that may possibly help to distract us. We can, most of all, be sure of no one interfering with us. We can just stand or sit in any of the cafés, and talk and look. There must be cafés for ten or a dozen nationalities— Maltese, West Indians, Somalis, West Africans, Turkish and Greek Cypriots, and so on—and we usually go in a West Indian or a Somali one. There's always a jukebox with their own pop music in it. One particular one we like has a dicegame on the ground floor and a club underneath it. Another has a football game we can play for sixpence. The Strasse has a reputation for all sorts of vice: but we never see much, and would be disappointed if we were merely tourists seeking it.

No, Cable Street for us is a place to come to remind us that other people are suffering life when most of London seems dead. It is, too, a place for outcasts, misfits, where we feel something in common, however else we differ.

Mostly we talk about women: and mostly about this cow Janine who's done Terry down, as Jenny did me down. This is the chief bond between us: as we have this need to talk and equally as we have this need to listen.

But we also talk about teaching, for instance, for he still teaches over at some grammar at Sidcup near where he used to live with her. We compare his experience with mine, so totally dissimilar though we teach only a few miles apart. And we talk about how education is so desperately old-fashioned, of such very low productivity, and of the waste, the waste, and of the ineffectual cosiness of our colleagues, of the other teachers, and of what we would ideally do in education. This breeds such frustration in us that in revolt, in desperation almost, we become like delinquent teachers in going to places like the Strasse and doing various other things (or thinking about doing them) which would blight our laughable teaching careers if they were known.

Anyway, we talk, we listen and watch, several nights a week. And I'll suddenly want to see some building or other, and off we will go in the Fiat, Terry talking perhaps, me listening and looking at the architecture on the way, or playing solo pontoon with car numbers. That's how it so often is. I'll say I want to see Wren's Observatory at Greenwich Park again, and we go: to find the Park is shut at that time of night, but we have a marvellous prospect across London by night. And to all sorts of other places we go on these night journeys, for all sorts of reasons, or non-reasons, or for no reasons, having coffee occasionally at anywhere we happen to find open: to save the loneliness, the oneness, of being in bed alone at night, for each of us.

There is a very good Greek Cypriot place about equidistant from Terry's and mine, up the Liverpool Road, and we often end up there. Georgiou seems to have a different waitress every time we go in: they get the sack if they won't sleep with him. They're never Cypriot girls, either, and we kid him about this, saying they all go about in total black as soon as they're sixteen, as though in mourning for a lost innocence. Georgiou's place has a steep flight of wooden steps down to it from the street, covered by an awning, and the outside walls have a vitriolite crazy mosaic all over them, shiny pastel colours and black. Inside, the walls have murals which incongruously incorporate the room's projections and abutments. Terry thinks they picture something like a decadent nineteenth-century Bari. I don't quite know what he means by this, as with a number of his remarks: they, like himself, are sort of offset to reality, as mine are, too, but it's a different offset. Anyway, one of the noble heads reminds me of Robert Graves, and there are Norman-type castles, and some blocks of what look like modern flats but which might equally be Roman *insulæ*.

Georgiou sells marvellous Turkish coffee, and great *shish-kebab*—flat, floury envelopes of bread stuffed with spitted veal, chopped onion, parsley, and tomato, with a segment of lemon to squeeze into it. We usually, almost as a ritual, have a coffee and a *kebab* each, and play the jukebox, which has mostly Greek popular music in it. Sometimes we will also have a *paklava*, or a *kataifi*, or a *galatopoureko*, to finish with, and play on the fruit machines

Georgiou has in the little barrel-vaulted room which forms a crosspiece to the longer shape of the main one. *ΑΠΑΓΟΡΕΥΕΤΑΙ Ο ΧΟROS—COSMAS* it warns, and perhaps fortunately we rarely feel like dancing anyway.

The curtains of the window beside the counter are always left undrawn to reveal a section of the wooden steps outside: this is Georgiou's private legshow, to which he is very partial.

So there we sit, Terry and I, in this eighteenth-century cellar, while the smart hairy Cypriot boys preen and look arrogantly in the mirrors, Londoners like us.

And we talk, talk, talk, talk, talk. As though it could make some difference.

* * * * *

You all must have been told about God in previous R.I. lessons with your own teacher, you must have talked about God as though it was certain that he existed, as though his existence was a fact. I want this morning briefly not to question the existence of God—the law wouldn't approve of my doing that in any case in this classroom—but I do want to ask some questions about a few of the things which follow from accepting, as we do, of course, in this classroom, that there is a God.

You have all been taught, for instance, that God is good, that God is love: yet from your own experience, limited as it is to your own twelve or thirteen years of life, you must all have seen that this is hardly likely to be true, or, if it is true at all, true only in a very special and in a very limited way. How can you think that God is good when you learn in History lessons about terrible wars which have killed thousands of people, and made thousands more, and even millions more, suffer? Some of which wars, like the Crusades, have been undertaken in God's name? If God created everything, must he not then have created war, as well? And disease, too, and suffering, and death, and poverty, and all the unpleasant things in the world? Can such a God be called good, then, can such a God be called the God of *love*? Perhaps only when he is being good, perhaps only when he is being loving?

You have been told, too, that he is a God who knows everything: *omniscient* is the word we use to mean 'knows everything', *om – ni – sci – ent*, it's a Latin word. I'll put it on the board. But does God know everything? *Everything*? Does he really? Everything that's going on, everything that there is? Does he know, for instance, how many specks of chalkdust there are on the board? Or in this classroom? Or in the school? Or in the whole world? And why should he be interested, anyway, in how many specks of chalkdust there are?

All these are really questions about what sort of a God he is, then, assuming, as we do, that he does exist; they are questions about what we can know about him. Is there any reason why he should not be a bad God, for instance, an evil God, if he made all the evil things in the world too? Do you think that he might actually have made a mess of creating the world, and that the bad things were mistakes he couldn't put right? Even if he was capable of thinking up the idea of creating the world, does that mean as well that he was capable of actually doing it? What if he saw that he'd bitten off more than he could chew, and

then just gave up the world as a bad job—or a bad joke—
and went off to try to do better somewhere else? Yet if he
is capable of better, why didn't he do it on earth? Perhaps
some of you know how, if you make a bad job of something,
then you hate it and everything connected with it. Is that
how God feels about us, and about the world? And has
he just deserted us, left us to get on as best we can in his
mess? Has he just gone away? Gone off in disgust, perhaps,
if not in hatred, to somewhere else, just not interested any
more in us? Or perhaps he is dead—how do we know that
he couldn't die, that he didn't die, that he couldn't be
dead?

You cannot, I cannot, no one can *know*, truly *know*, the
answers to these questions. What is certain is that you are
here on this earth and that there are some good things and
some bad things, and that you enjoy the good things and
that you suffer the bad things. This is what is called the
human predicament, or the human condition, or the human
situation. 'Predicament', 'condition', and 'situation', in
this case are all words which mean something like 'fix',
'jam', 'awkward position'. And being human as you all are
means that you are in this 'awkward fix' of enjoying the
good things whilst at the same time having to suffer the
bad things, whether or not anyone or any God created it.
Whether or not, remember, whether or not.

Faced with this human situation, then, what do you do?
What can you do? The main thing is to behave with dignity, dignity: human dignity is your greatest refuge, your
greatest comfort. *Accept* the human situation, do not go
blaming the bad things on to God, or, equally, thanking
him for the good things; accept that fire burns you and
that stone is hard when you run up against, come into
contact with, either of them, accept that wom ... that

other people are treacherous to you and hurt you: and remember that fire is good for warmth, for instance, and
pavements for walking on, and other people—often the
same people—are also kind and warm and loving sometimes. You can accept it all with dignity, dignity, the
greatest, the most godlike, of all human qualities. You can
accept responsibility for everything, but absolutely everything, that happens to you: for who else is there to do so?

And call nothing human, inhuman: this man in the
papers who cut up his wife and sent her in bits through the
post to her relatives, for instance, is not inhuman. How
could his actions, being those of a human being, be called
inhuman? They are encompassed by humanity, they even
have a comic side to them, and the comic goes a long way
towards making up for anything. He did no harm to you,
did he, nor to me? What unthinking people mean by calling him 'inhuman' is really that he offended against the
best in humanity, that he failed to achieve the good, the
best, of which humanity is capable. But he's still a human
being, in the same condition as you are, in the same condition as I am. He lost his dignity, you could say of him
and of his actions, he could not accept the suffering with
dignity: and that is perhaps the lowest state of humanity,
that is certainly a crime against humankind.

In the end, all you are left with is the dignity of humankind.

You have heard me ask a great many questions this
morning, and heard me give one answer. You must go
away and think about what I have said for yourselves. Some
of my questions may seem silly to you, some may not even
seem to be real questions at all, to you. What you must
not do is to think that these *are* real questions and yet still
think you know anything about God. In other words, don't

let there be a difference between what you believe because you have been told it, and what you have seen and felt for yourselves. Whether you decide there is or is not a God, or whether you refuse to decide, face up to being human, to being in the human predicament, and accept with dignity everything, but everything, that happens to you in any way whatsoever.

And think, tomorrow morning when you're singing the hymn in assembly, think what the words *mean*, and whether you believe them to be true: and, if you do not believe them to be true, then think why you are singing them.

*   *   *   *   *

They had had to walk on the third day, but by then they had arrived: to Fishguard it had been easy, a lucky straight hitch, and then the boat to Cork with a night's loving and sleeping in a cabin that was like their first home, transitory as it was; then walking through the coldmorning city, and three lifts to Tralee by way of Macroom and Killarney; and finally, on that third day, the walking north after a bus to Dingle.

They had had rain about three o'clock, when they were walking along an unmetalled road parallel to the sea. There had been mountains like hooded Fathers rising to their south, and a sea like tarnished hammered pewter in Brandon Bay to their north. This had been the first rain they had had on the whole journey from London, and they felt that to complain about it would have been ungrateful.

Lead-underbellied clouds had come from the north-west, had cut off up to the haunches the purple mountains and had foreshortened the horizon. They had brought umbrellas, firstly as a gimmick for lifts, but then they had been glad to use them seriously.

They had decided that it would be as well to pitch their tent at the first place suitable, because of the set-in rain, rather than go on farther eastwards as they had at first intended. They had come down a path towards a lough and had turned inland along it: everywhere the land had been sodden and marshy, with peat digs here and there. They had walked about a mile alongside the lough without finding a large enough area of firm grass, drinking water from the bitter lough to ease unusual thirsts, before they had decided to turn back towards the sea. A stream had led out of the lough, down through striated rocks, and amongst these rocks they had found a small area of thick, close grass, green as spring, as unexpected as if it had been a hotel, and more welcome, where they had set their camp. When they were warm and comfortable they had realised that their love had come through its most severe trying yet: that miserable walk in the heavy rain with no knowledge of where they would that night sleep.

The lower slopes of the mountains at their backs had been enforested, the regular patterns of the plantations counterpointing the wildness of the summits' outlines against the sky. From the skin of earth and grass had protruded enormous rock outcrops, red like contusions when the sun in the evening had fallen upon them.

They had spent six days at this place, which had no name on their maps: but they had called it Balgy, for no reason other than that it had come to them, Balgy. They had built a kitchen area protected by rocks, and dug a pit in which to bury their detritus, and had defined an area where they could comfortably and civilisedly defecate, and had found a thicket where they could collect wood for a fire.

Gneiss had been exposed in two great slabs at acute angles, the fault cut wider by the stream, the sides showing glacial striation. They had sketched the mountains, and had talked, had cooked and eaten enormous meals, and had never been as close. They had designed and drawn a house to be built for them over this stream, founded on the gneiss, inspired by Frank Lloyd Wright but more beautiful than his *Falling Water*, they had thought, and they had called it *Above the Fault*.

On the ninth day they had left their Balgy, regretfully, and had walked eastwards to Tralee, twenty miles in that one day, on that warm day, and with heavy packs: and this journey and its physical exhaustion had drawn them the closest they were ever to be, for its length. Well before they had reached London they had both known that they had passed the pitch of their loving.

THREE: Development

The Fight

One day of last term I had a fight with a second year boy, quiet by accident I threw a stone and caught him on his head, I at once apologised but this wasnt enough for him he struck me, I hit back and hurt my fist. After the fight was over I went down the hospital and had a brocken finger, my arm was put in plaster. And next day the boy laughed at me so I hit him on the head with my plaster and squirted ink from my pen onto his face and went to my form room and I was sent to mr. Harrison and he made us be friends and from that day on we were friends. Next day we had a friendly fight and I busted is nose. FIN

A Night Out

The night was cold, with slight patches of fog or mist surrounding the city. As the night drew on rime formed on the back street roads, there was too much traffic on the main roads for frost to form.

My friend Jim and I went for a ride on a bus to New Oxford Street, after looking in the shop windows we went round to the "Moulin Rouge", it was not open so we went for a walk around the back streets, such as Drury Lane and Grape Street. After walking back to Bloomsbury Square we got on a bus, in this three Greeks or Italians were sitting next to two girls, one turned round and licked his lips, I don't know what he meant but when most of the people had left he started kissing her.

When we got off I got a dirty look from one of the men, I think it was because I kept on looking at them in the bus.

We saw that same woman with another man a few nights later and I made my own conclusion from that. She was a prostitute Many people do those sort of things, Just for a kick, and it is on the increase. Now, instead of the girls walking the street, they stand on doorsteps, or the doors of night clubs, some even stand on their own step! Most people who do those things are between twenty and forty. Teenagers do it for nothing!

What a scrap.

One day as my mates and I were coming home from a long game of football we all stopped to buy an ice-cream. As we waited our turn at the van we saw some toughs walking towards us. Mind out the way so we can get our ice-creams first they said. Why should we, we all said. And in reply they said "Because we said so. "Oh move along you bunch of jungle bunnies," as most of them were darkies. The ice-cream man laughed at this remark. "What did you call us," they said. "Jungle Bunnies," we answered. You ought to get you're ear-oles cleaned. You might be able to hear better. As soon as we had said this the toughs charged us. I landed a punch on an on-running darkie which made his nose even more flat. I then turned round to see how my mates were getting on. They were doing okay as I see one punch one of the toughs in the eye. The bundle went on for quite a while. All the time the ice-cream man was laughing his head off. "What do you think you're laughing at," I said. At that moment everybody stopped fighting. We all started throwing stones and anything in hands reach. We then after made friends with the toughs.

The Killer Master

On the first day back from the holidays we had a new French teacher, he had a sort of a dull look with spec's hanging over his nose. When he first took us for french I hated his guts. He set lots of homework, and if he did not get the homework he had a size ten slipper with which he applied maximum pain. When he was puting work on the Blackboard for us to do we used to fire ink pellets at his back. At the end of the lesson his back was covered in ink. For this he called us all back one night and asked who fire them. A deadly Huss fell over the class as he walked up and down the gang ways. Suddenly the boy behind me said something to the boy next to him. The Master in a

deadly rage got hold of the boy by his hair, and dragged
him to the front of the class where he brutally hit him the
boy fell to the floor moaning then master kicked him, the
class by then were shouting their heads off. With that he
walked out of the class and that was the last we ever saw
of him

*   *   *   *   *

"2. *The Development of
the Gothic Style seen as an
Immanent Process. The im-
provement of Romanesque
groin-vaults came about as
a result of a rational con-
sideration of the geometric
construction of the arches
and the surfaces of the cells;
the building technique em-
ployed, that is, the centering; their statics, both during and after construction;
and also the economic problems which they presented.
But all these considerations
always went hand in hand
with the aim of producing
an aesthetically satisfying
result. The changes had nothing to do with the Cru-
sades, which began only*

later, or with the liturgy, or with philosophy. The architects were intent simply upon making necessary improvements. As far as can be reconstructed, this was a process of trial and error which led to the replacement of diagonal, wooden centering arches by the stone cintre permanent, *that is the rib.*

Here, the question must indeed have arisen as to whether the architectural patrons of this time, the clergy, were in agreement with the introduction of this innovation; but this question can be ignored for the moment. The development which was described in the first part of this book shows that the rib-vault, in its turn, was further improved by a combination of rational considerations and aesthetic criticism, which resulted in the introduction of pointed arches, first over the four sides of each bay, and finally in the diagonals also. This process, too, was an im-

manent, or an internal one. Just as master-masons did not determine the form of the liturgy or indulge in metaphysics, so the clergy did not build scaffolding, or draw designs for arches or for the profiles of ribs. These are different spheres, different jobs, requiring special skills, and it need hardly be said that no amount of knowledge of metaphysics can help one to build a rib-vault, and that on the other hand the ability of an architect to build a vault cannot help him to decide whether general . . ."

————No, but I will do!

————. . . then he came round to my place and you know what my Dad is, I mean, he wouldn't . . .

————Rah!

————. . . than I thought it would be, just went in easy like, and . . .

Get out! Out! What d'you mean by coming into my class and making such a hell of a row? Eh? Eh! Get out and line up outside, and be dead quiet until I tell you

Damn! Knew I shouldn't have started another section. Bloody sharp on the breaks here. Not a minute over all the week.

to come in. DEAD quiet, d'you understand?

——Albie'll 'ave t' go if 'e's goin' t' be like this all the time, 'e'll 'ave t' go!

——'E's got 'ead on 'im like a side of bacon, en 'e?

I said QUIET! QUIET! You! What was that about bacon?

——Nothing.

Well whatever it was, keep it for later.

——Albert's got new suedes on.

——Cor, dig them broffel-creepers!

Marvellous phrase. Try not to laugh.

That's enough!

——No, but I will do.

Right, you, once more and you'll get thumped.

——You ent allowed to 'it kids.

And you're not allowed to talk when I tell you not to. You break rules, and then so shall I.

Perfect answer. But works only once, usually. Next time?

Right. Now file in quietly and sit down. Without talking!

——No, but I will do.

All right, little one, come out here. You did hear me say 'no talking', didn't you?

I asked you a question! Did you hear me say 'no talking'?
——No, but I w ... oh! You ent sposed to 'it kids on the 'ead!

Just go and sit down and don't let me hear another word from you unless I ask for it. And what's your name? What's your name!
——Langley.
Langley.

——'E'll 'ave to go, then, them suedes 'n' all, the lot!
Right, settle down, I

Stupid truculence. Have to hit him now.

⟶Eyes narrowly, skin very white, hands just like trotters and dirty, nicotine-stained.⟵

All violence rebounds on society. He'll take it out on another kid. Or on something.

But what hurt did I just now pass on? It must stop somewhere, but why with me? Or is there a constant quantity of violence in the world, continually circulating?

know it's the last lesson of the day and you can't wait to get home, but first you're going to listen very carefully to a Geology lesson. What's Geology? Langley? Anyone else?

——It's to do with dirt and stones and stuff like that.

Yes, that's nearly right. Geology is the study of earth and stones and everything that goes to make up the world except for the living things like plants and animals. And ourselves. Have you learnt anything about this subject before?

——No.

——No.

——Don't want to now.

——No.

Not in Geography lessons? Nothing at all?

Nor can I, for that matter.

Then I'll have to start right from the beginning. You all know what stone is, and that there are different

Thick. Or resentful. And. Can't get any response today. Either. Haven't tried very hard. Guilt. But tiredness. C-stream, too, christ knows what the H-stream must be like!

Even that assuming too much? Cynical, cynical.

sorts of stone—you can see that in the houses you live in: there's the slate on the roof, and the stone of the window cills and the doorstep, and some of you may have marble mantelpieces, and the bricks are made of clay, which is really very tiny pieces of stone mixed up with other things that I'll tell you about in due course. Coal is yet another kind of stone. All these different sorts of stones came from underneath the ground—that is, from underneath the grass and earth. In some places the stone sticks out of the earth and only has to be cut or broken off to be used, but in other places men have to dig or quarry for it. Anyone seen a quarry when they've been on holiday in the country?

More likely Coade round here, or some other composition.

Nothing. This class is a nothing.

No? Well, next time you do go out of London keep your eyes open for quarries. Anyway, when you look at the country you see that most of it is covered

And I'm a nothing teacher.

with grass and soil. But this is only a thin topcoat, like the skin on a rice-pudding, say, while underneath lies rock, solid rock.
——Give me that rice-pudding rock, daddy-o.

Quick enough when they want to be. Then the teaching has been at fault. Mine must not be.

Right, joke over. In Geography you must have been told of all the different kinds of countryside there are in Great Britain—mountains, barren heaths, uplands, wide fertile plains—and the importance of Geology is that each of these regions, and the others . . .

Sentence getting tortuous.

The reason why each region is different from the others is because of the different kind of rock or stone which lies underneath the soil, where there is soil, that is.

Too simple for fourteen-year-olds? Can't be if they've never done any before. Constant problem.

Now, Geology is a science, and in the sciences one of our chief methods of going about things is by classification. That is to say, we put things in order, we make them tidy, by grouping them into their different kinds. Take out your rough notebooks, and copy down the following different sorts or classes of rocks.

Aristotle.

And you can do it without talking!

They don't like that. Means they'll have to work.

How I hate this perpetual nagging. Ninety percent of teaching is nagging. Someone won't have a pencil.

——Mr. Albert, I need a new roughbook.

Thick, virginal, sensuous pile of new books. A small pleasure.

Here.
Now, has everyone got a pencil? Or something to . . . with which to write?

Amazing. Now what to say next, no respite?

Put the heading 'Geology' just as I'm spelling it on the board.
Now, different sorts of

stone have different ages, and I'm going to start with the oldest. The earth was once a ball of flame, its surface a mass of material so hot that we can hardly imagine it. The sun is like this today, and the centre of the earth is, too. The heat was so great that it melted . . .

——'Ow does 'e know about the sun and the middle of the earth? 'As 'e bin there?

True, how do I bloody well know? Might have been a ball of shit for all I know, a ball of stinking shit. So? You don't have to believe in anything to teach it?

. . . the rocks so that . . . Just be quiet and listen, for the moment, and you'll have a chance to ask questions later.

To which I shall be pleased to invent answers.

Now, this heat was so enormous that it melted the rocks, it made them so hot that they flowed like water. You've all seen solder when it's melted, the way it flows, well that's what happened to the rocks of the earth, in the beginning . . .

Biblical. And who said that was the beginning anyway?

Now, those rocks which were melted in this way are the oldest, and as they gradually cooled they set into shapes that ...

These rocks we call igneous rocks, the oldest ones that were once very hot, in the beginning. Igneous is a word which means 'fiery'. So copy down this word igneous and the number 'one' against it.

This is the first class of rocks, the igneous rocks, which were formed by great heat many millions of years ago—about five thousand million years ago, scientists seem to think. So copy all this down, now.

It's about bloody time they gave us something less primitive than blackboard and chalk.

Right, Langley, why are you talking again? As soon as my back is turned you talk.

I ought to clobber him again. They'll think I'm weak if I don't. But don't want to hit him. So shan't.

Just get on with what you were told to do. How

far have you got? Get on
with it!

You haven't done much.

*Igneous, igneous, 'ideous
rocks.*

⌐ *Soft, starched collar, bitten nails, squat.* ⌐

You haven't even star-
ted!
——Ent got no pencil.

⌐*Hair fine, saffron mist,
neck scarred.* ⌐

I asked ten minutes ago
whether you all had some-
thing to write with! Go out
and get one from my desk.

Why can't you get on?
Laziness!

⌐*Eyes like grapes, mouth
a melon segment.* ⌐

——'E'll 'ave t' go.
What was that?
——I'll 'ave t'go to the
toilet. Please, sir, Mr.
Albert?
No. Wait.

*They always ask twice if
they really want to.*

Now: have you all done
that? Come on then!
Now what makes ig-
neous rocks different from
the other sorts? How can
you specially tell? Well, first
of all, igneous rocks are very
hard, very hard indeed. And
they are often shiny, as well,
if you break a piece and look

at a surface that has not been made dull by the weather. This is because igneous rocks are made up of crystals, which are shiny themselves, lots of crystals of all different sizes. The sorts of crystals in each different igneous rock . . .

Doubt if anyone is following. My fault. Know what I want to say, but haven't prepared the lesson well enough to say it effectively. Guilt. But if all my spare time spent preparing lessons shouldn't have time for designing. And I am after all an architect, not a teacher, a creator, not a passer-on.

. . . make the difference between each sort. That is, some have crystals like felspar, mica, or quartz . . .

Useless. Abandon it.

Right now. I've given you two ways you can tell igneous rocks—they're very hard, and they're shiny when you break them. Now who can tell me the name of an igneous rock? Come on, think. Think.
——Sarfend Rock?

Quite funny.

And your name? Name!
——Gloria Stenning.

Please don't speak again unless you put up your hand and are asked to speak.

Bathos! Stock response— just bloody ludicrous. They should have laughed more. Don't tell you how to teach a class like this. At least, they tell you it is ultimately the Head's responsibility, you can go to him. But what if the Head doesn't give a damn? Didn't back my authority yesterday when I sent a boy to him.

——No, but I will do!

Langley again. This must be a stock phrase, one he trots out hopefully. Perhaps it once made kids laugh. Once in twenty times it will be hilarious: that's the time, that once, I've got to watch out for.

Friend Langley . . .

The shock approach.

. . . stuffit!
——Oooh, Mr. Albert sir!
——Oooh!
——You try!
——No, but I will do!
——Ooh, and he's supposed to be a teacher, too.

Not supposed to be human if you're a teacher.

Lesson appalling. For cris-sake pull it together.

Right! If you don't settle down and listen you'll find yourselves here after school until six o'clock.

The only sanction that may have some effect.

——You can't keep kids in more than half an hour.
——It's a rule.
——The L.C.C. says so.

The bastards know it all!

Can't I keep you in? Just watch me! And I've already explained that if you break rules, then so shall I.

Some effect.

Now: igneous rocks. I asked you if you knew the names of any rocks which were very hard and shiny.
——Sir?

⌐*Indian, thin face, oiled hair, intelligent eyes.* ⌐

Yes?
——Is one of them granite, sir?
Yes, indeed, granite is one of them. That's the one I was hoping most of you would know. What's your name?
——Navin Bhatia, sir.
Very good, Bhatia. How many of you others had

heard of granite? Come on, don't be lazy, put your hands up if you'd ever heard the word before.

I'm surprised at you not having heard of granite before, Langley. After all, your head's made of it. ———Ha. Ha.

A dozen of them.

Sarcasm, least effective and most vicious weapon, they tell you. But least easy to avoid, and most enjoyable.

Well, those of you who had heard of granite now know that it is a rock formed by intense heat many millions of years ago. You can see granite very often in London, because many buildings, especially big public buildings like banks and some offices, are faced with it. That is, a thin layer of granite is used to cover the brick or nowadays ferro-concrete structure. We call this thin facing layer 'ashlar'.

Illegitimately: form should be honest, should be honestly exposed.

Granite can be polished to a very high, shiny, that is, finish, and it is found in many different colours. In some places it is almost white, in others it is all shades of grey, green, a kind of blue, pink, deep red, brown and black. There's a particularly lovely grey-blue one which comes from Penmaenmawr in North Wales, which is . . .

Irrelevant.

Another place you can often see granite in all sorts of different colours is in cemeteries, where, because it is . . .

——Ooh!

——Eerh!

——You bin wandrin' round any cemeteries lately?

——My dad just 'ad wood.

——'E's right orf it.

Ignore. Louder.

. . . because granite is such a very hard stone I suppose people think their names cut in it will last that much longer.

Bloody stupid remark. Must go over and see Zulf and his fearful cemetery this week.

But granite is not the only igneous rock, though it is the most commonly used one . . . .

Definite evidence for that remark? None. Never mind.

There are some places where the crystals that go to make up igneous rocks are found in more or less pure states, where you get layers or seams or strata of almost pure quartz, or felspar or mica. Then, too, there are different impurities which give you different sorts of igneous rock. Two of these other sorts are basalt and gneiss. Basalt and gneiss: spelt like . . .
——Basil is nice?

Name? What's your name? You! I know it was you! And stand up! Name?
——Stenning.

You can't hold your tongue any more than your female namesake over here, can you?
——She's my sister.

You don't look like twins.
——We're not twins.

Oh.

Don't make stupid remarks,

On.

I'll get that fucking kid and beat . . . No, I won't.
⇀*Orange sweater, overgrown it, flopping hair, unwashed look, twists lips.*↽

What a bloody stupid, trite, readymade euphemism!

Two in the same year? Have to be bloody quick off the mark to get two in the same year. Must have been got at as soon as she'd had the first.

Stenning, or you'll find yourself in trouble.
———Ha-ha-ha.

Pointless threat. Deserved
derision. Just look at them
threateningly.

Basalt and gneiss. This
g is silent as in gnat. So now
we know three igneous
rocks: granite, basalt, and
gneiss, all of which were
formed by the action of heat
at a very early stage in the
earth's history.

Sheer bloody repetition of
teaching gets me. Once I've
learnt something I want to
go on, I want to build on it,
not go on repeating it.

Granite is the only one
used widely as a building
material. In an unpolished
state it is used for kerbs and
gutters. The kerbs and gutters of the street outside are
made of granite. Basalt is
often too hard to use for
building, and is chiefly
known for the spectacular
natural effects it creates
at the Giant's Causeway
in Northern Ireland, for
instance, and at Fingal's
Cave on the island of Staffa
in Scotland. Anyone ever

Is it?

been to either of these places? No? The composer Mendelssohn wrote a well-known piece of music, an overture, called after Fingal's Cave. Perhaps I'll play a record of it to you in a music lesson when we next have one. Well, as the basalt in these places cooled it split into interesting shapes: regular shapes. Into hexag ... into six-sided columns.

Gneiss is hardly used at all in building, mainly because it is laminated or foliated. That is, it is made up of thin layers which fairly easily split apart. Not that it isn't hard, however, for it is, but its strength lies only one way. You could build a house on gneiss, however, if the layers went the right way.

Above the Fault, Falling Water, Balgy, Jenny, oh Jenny!

Now: I happen to have with me a piece of gneiss, that I brought back with me from the west of Ireland, and I'm going to pass it round the class now so that you can see what it looks like. This was part of a huge outcrop of gneiss and I knocked this piece off it as a sort of souvenir, you might say . . .

——Albie's knocked off some ice . . .

Quiet! Quiet! When it comes to you, feel how hard it is, and you can see the crystals glinting in it, and you can see the layers as well. You won't be able to split any off, though, as the piece is too small to get enough leverage on it. Right, until the piece comes to you, get on with writing down from the board these three types of igneous rock, and against each one write down what you can remember of what I've said about it.

Which isn't much. But a respite for me. Sit down.

We came back from collecting wood, yes, dragging branches over the peat and turf, and reached our place by the fault just after rain began, laughing as we ran

*the last stretch, and fell in-
side the spread entrance of
the tent. Soft filtered light,
unnaturally green through
the light canvas. Out of
breath, leaving the firewood
out in the rain, and we made
love, beautifully, suddenly;
remember Jenny's almost-
closed eyes and the half-
caught intense sounds she
made, and the way she held
me within her, and the way
I surpassed myself in pleas-
ing her, and she, me. And—
oh god!—we ran out naked
as we were into the rain and
down into the deep pool
below the fault and swam
the four and a half strokes
there were room for again
and again and—oh god,
how every thought of Jenny
hurts, how such pleasure
has now become such pain,
in the remembering, yet is
still pleasure, the greatest I
ever, the pleasure and the
pain inextricably together!
Shouting and holding each
other, so close. So close, and
running around in the rain,
laughing that we would dry*

——No, but I will do!

——Shush!

——Albie'll 'ear you!

——Not 'im—'e's miles away.

——'E's got that dozy look.

——Dreamy Albie.

——Ma famly? You bin sayin' fings about ma famly?

——I'll get you, just you wait!

——Watch it, cocker, or you'll be 'avin' a visit from the Corps.

——I'm terrified.

——Read it out to 'er.

——No, shush, Albert'll see it.

——I don't care. 'E wouldn't get it off me anyway.

——The Corps ...

——Go on, read it, ent it funny ...

What the hell d'you

ourselves, and seeing, needing, once more, and making love again, this time on that just-yielding bed of grass, this time laughing where the other was serious, this time lingering and drawn where the first was swift and compulsive, this time so conscious, civilised, where the first was natural, uncontrolled, this time so lastingly satisfying where the first was immediately fulfilling. Ah, Jenny, oh god, god, god! My love, that's it, my love, you can never go back, that high, yet how I miss it! The love! Singular, only, only one, the love, the love. Not so much her, Jenny, but the love, for there were— were there?—bad things— weren't there?—about her I don't miss. But do I, were they part of the love? They must have been, yes, all part of the love, part of the pain and the pleasure and the joy, the joyous in the rain. and the suffering ...
Bloody noise!

mean by making so much noise! Silence! You, there, what's on that piece of paper that you find so irresistibly funny?

Up, get it. Up, certainly, got a stand on, no bloody wonder ...

——Oh, Albie's got lead in 'is pencil.

Give it to me!

Girl, my grip is a hundred times yours so don't struggle. Give it to—give me that piece of paper!

Thank you.

"Jeanette Parsons, 3C. When I was young I had no sence I took a girl behind the frence I gave her a shilling she was willing I gave her a pound she laid on the ground. I gave her a spack she open her prat and there I planted my union Jack."
Not even funny. Except about the flag. Very few spelling errors, though.

Kind of you to put your name on it, Jeanette Parsons. I suppose you're proud of it, are you? Stand up.

⌐Bottle-red, good teeth, not wearing bra.⌐ Not the same girl I took it from.

And the girl who was reading this? What's your name?
——Lily Stanley.

⌐Hooked nose, thin hair, eyes watering.⌐ Don't know how some parents can name so badly. Repeating terminal sounds.

Well, Jeanette Parsons and Lily Stanley, I shall report this affair to the Headmaster.
——Ooooh, I'm frightened!

Who will do fuck-all about it.

Just SHUT UP!
Now, has everyone looked at the piece of gneiss, the stone I sent round? Who's got . . . who has it at the moment?

Here! I was a silly bastard to let these thieving sods get their hands on it.

I asked a question! Who has the stone I sent round?

Not bloody funny, that stone is practically the only thing I have tangible of Jenny, she hardly ever wrote me letters, there was no occasion to, we saw each other so often.

Please don't let's play games like little children,

children's games. Who's got
my stone?
——Albert's got 'is 'ard up.
——Just for 'is bleedin'
stone.

Right! I'm just not
messing about with chil-
dren. And I certainly don't
want to punish the infant
who is playing games. I'm
going outside the door for
just long enough for someone to bring out the stone
and put it on my desk. If it's
not there when I come back,
then we're in for a long session tonight. I doubt if any
of you will get home before
dark. You'll miss a lovely
summer's evening. Unless
my stone is on that desk
within one minute from
now!

Not fucking much.

*Cold, just as they say, anger.
Jenny's stone, my stone,
from Balgy, nice gneiss she
kept on calling it, gnice
neiss, so sweetly the words
became a poem, for me, a
love-poem, and the piece
broken for the two of us,
one part each, for her, for
me, a mistake to break it, a*

mistake, a symbol, a symbolic mistake, like so many others. All the others.

What will I do if they don't give it back? They'll certainly be kept in. But I want to get off myself very smartly tonight to see Terry. I could search them all. Not the girls. That means I would have to call in a woman teacher. No. Oh, the bastards!

Give them twenty seconds more.

Right!

The repetitious right or wrong. Thank the christ, it's there, covered in ink, but there. Wipe it carefully with blotting-paper, I must wash it when I get home, salve it, though wash off her touch, kiss, on my stone, our stone, the only stone, the only thing I have left, my Jenny-stone.
They're all expecting me to make some comment. The bastards,   the . . . waste. Waste. Snap.

Igneous rocks in Great Britain are mainly found in the Highlands of Scotland, the Lake District, North Wales, and in the moorland areas of Devon and Cornwall. Thus these areas represent geologically the oldest parts of the country, as far as we can tell. But long after the formation of these rocks the world became very cold—why, we don't really know—and large parts of it were covered with ice, great icesheets and huge glaciers. Glaciers are great masses of ice which fill whole valleys and move slowly towards the sea. Now, all except the southern part of Britain was covered in this ice at this time—it was about a million years ago, and is called the Pleistocene Age—but not London, that is, the ice . . .

——The Plasticine age?

. . . stopped some miles north of London, and has thus not affected the nature of the country as it has in the areas which were . . .

——Ooooh! You . . .

I shall belt that bastard as hard as I can round the ear. Enjoyably.

... covered with ice. Yes?
You were going to call me
something? To address me?
——What you got such a
temper for, then? Ooooh!

All you have to do at
the moment is to listen.
Then you don't get hurt.

This ice had several
effects. For one, it was of
such enormous weight that
it ground down everything
beneath it; and there were
often mountains covered by
it, that is, it was often so
deep that it covered even
mountains. And it carried
south with it all sorts of
rocks from the northern
parts from which it came.
In this way, you will find
igneous rock, often large
boulders, in areas where
the underlying rock is not
igneous at all. In some areas,
these boulders have often
been used for building—in
Wiltshire, for instance,
which is mainly chalk,
though there the boulders
are of sandstone and are not
igneous. They are called
'sarsens', or, sometimes,

Two of them.

'greywethers', and Stonehenge, for instance, is made of them. The word 'sarsen' means, is the same as, 'Saracen', and was used for many sorts of stranger or foreigner: thus 'sarsens' are strange boulders, ones which are out of place, are not at home, in the place where they are found, having been brought there, as I told you, by the action of glaciers.

Myself, a sarsen amongst dirt and stuff like that.

Right, then, write down these further notes just as I put them on the board.

Got them at last. At last. Not even talking while my back's turned. And my stone comfortingly in my pocket, back again, hell, I don't know what ... But I got it back.

——Thank god for that!
——Aaah!
——Raaah!
——Fffffh!
——Rah! Rah!

Soddit, there goes the bell! Just as I'd got them.

All right, that's enough. Quiet! You can't be more glad than I am that the lesson's over. Put your books away—after finishing the

Wrong order.

sentence you're writing, of course. I'll finish putting up the notes next week.

——Next week's half-term.

I also intend next time to talk about the other classes of rock: sandstone, which is made up of very tiny... Look, if you want to get home before midnight, you'd better keep quiet!

——You won't keep me in, Albert, boy!

Too tired to fight any more. Ignore.

Sandstone, which is closely compressed grains of sand cemented together naturally, and limestone, which is made up of the shells of millions of former sea-creatures, again highly compressed.

——Huh!

I don't know how far we shall be able to get in Geology. It rather depends on how long Mr. Burroughs is away. But with what ...

——Bunny'll be away a long time, mate, don't you worry about that!

——Yeah.

——A long time.

That's enough for one day

for me, for crissake. Get rid.

Right! That girl there can go. She's been sitting quietly ready to go.

Always makes the others sit up and shut up.

Right. You can all go.
——Rah! Rah!

Mistake! Mistake! Soon as I said it! The bastards! Too late to bring them back now. Get them right under from the beginning next time. Try.

——Albie'll defenly 'ave t' go, y'know, defenly, just like Bunny.
——Stuffit, stuffit!
——'E's kep' us three minutes more'n 'e should 'ave.
——'Is 'ead is made of gneiss but it ent nice.
——No, but I will do!
——Granny and basil ent nice.
——All that fuss for a bit of stone!
——Up the Corps!
——Stuffit!

And only let them go one at a time, too.

——'e's bin sayin' fings about ma famly?
——Rahh!

Now where's my pen?

——If 'e's bin sayin' fings about the Corps 'e'll get one up 'is jacksie.
——Sir, could I ask you a question, please?

⌐Indian, thin, intelligent eyes.⌐

Certainly. I'm sorry, I forget your name?

——Navin Bhatia, sir.

Don't think he's getting at me.

Yes, I'm sorry, Bhatia, yes. What is it you want to ask?

Only one to show some interest. The one they say makes it all worth while. Yes, yet at the same time feel disappointed that I can't dismiss the whole class as bastards.

——I was very interested in this Geology, sir, and I am wondering whether you can recommend any books for further perusal?

Speaks well, and oh so politely.

Yes, certainly I can, Navin, and I'm glad that you're interested. I'll give you a list of some books which you can borrow from the library—the school library may have some of them—is there a school library? Have you seen a pen? A Parker fountain pen, black . . .

Where's my pen?

Using it when this class came in. Making notes from Frankl. Oh, christ, went out of the room! Some bastard has knocked off my pen! Oh, oooorh! Makes me feel ill, ill.

Look, Bhatia, d'you mind if we leave this until tomorrow? I'll give you a list then. Or if your usual teacher comes back then I'll post it to you. I really will.

——I think Mr. Burroughs is likely to be away for some time, sir.

Why?

——He seemed very . . . ill, sir, the last day he was here.

Oh? Well, in that case I may be here a week or more then. Anyway, I'll see you tomorrow or the next time you're due to have me.

Oh, god, the thought!

——Yes, sir. Thank you, Mr. Albert, sir.

Now, make sure my pen's not on the floor. Or anywhere else. No. One final look on the table. I didn't leave it in the book, did I— Oh! Fuck! No, fuck the bastards, they've spattered it with ink! They've befouled my Frankl! Oh, no, no, no! NO!

* * * * *

229 SHEPHERDESS WALK
LONDON N.1.

ATTENTION! MR. ALBERT!
I UNDERSTAND FROM MY DAUGHTER ROBERTA
THAT SHE ASKED PERMISSION TO LEAVE CLASS
ROOM TO GO TO TOILET AND WAS REFUSED.
PLEASE SEE THAT THIS DOES NOT OCCUR
AGAIN——
I DONT APPRECIATE THIS ATTITUDE——WAIT-
ING FIVE MINUTES CAN CAUSE UNPLEASANT-
NESS THAT EVEN YOU SHOULD UNDERSTAND.

YOURS FAITHFULLY
J. PROBBIT (MRS).

"Since none but the human ſpecies are properly ſubject to this menſtrual flux of blood (although there are ſome animals who, at the time of their vernal copulation, diſtil a ſmall quantity of blood from their genitals), and ſince the body of the male is always free from the like diſcharge, it has been a great inquiry in all ages, what ſhould be the cauſe of this ſanguine excretion peculiar to the fair ſex? To this effect the attraction of the moon, which is known to raiſe the tides of the ſea, has been accuſed in all ages; others have referred it to a ſharp ſtimulating humour, ſecreted in the genital parts themſelves, the ſame which is the cauſe of venereal diſeaſe. But if the moon was the parent of this effect, it would appear in all women at the ſame time; which is contrary to experi-ence, ſince there is never a day in which there are not many women ſeized with this flux; nor are there fewer in the decreaſe than the increaſe of the moon. As to any ſharp ferment ſeated in the uterus or its parts, it will be always inquired for in vain; where there are none but mild mucous juices, and where venery, which expels all thoſe juices, neither increaſes nor leſſens the menſtrual flux; and women deny that, during the time of their menſes, they have any increaſed deſire of venery; ſeeing at that time moſt of the parts are rather pained and languid; and the ſeat of venereal pleaſure is rather in the entrance of the pudendum than in the uterus, from which laſt the menſes flow."

from: *A Syſtem of Anatomy and Phyſio-*
logy from the Lateſt and Beſt
Authors. Arranged as nearly as
the nature of the work would
admit in the Order of the Lec-
tures delivered by the Profeſſor
of Anatomy in the Univerſity of
Edinburgh. 1787. *Volume III,*
page 11.

*   *   *   *   *

...where she wanted it, she wanted it, and I under-
neath holding her, and holding her, and holding her, and
wanting her, and enormous, and o – o – o – o – o, turning,
o – o – o, and it won't, won't, won't, she will, she will, she
wants, it, won't, enormous, enormous, again, again, again,
again, again, again, again, again, again, o – o – o....
...o–o–o–o–o. White, white. Then blueyellow-white. Pattern, lamp, greenwhite shade, Pollard, Astrophel and Stella, The White Goddess, the sovereign of my,

the white, the suspicious chair, greywhite trousers mine, the cupboard, oh! Damn! Another day! Another white day to waste on school, oh, the day, another until the day to be got through, to be suffered—no! No! Whitsun! No school! Half-term for Whitsun, three heartfelt cheers for the descent of the Holy Ghost on the day of Pentecost! Ah, rest, rest, relax, sleep until two, if I like, courtesy of my mate the Holy Apparition. Whitsun, and no bleeding kids! For this relief much thanks, much thanks!

So: waking again with this enormous tonk on, it ought to be relieved, too tired to last night, but anyway it seems to happen every night, every morning I wake with the most almighty jack. This is not good, I can think of better uses, still it's at least reassuring of my continued potence, no need to resort to Damaroids yet, remember after Jenny smashed me, for three weeks I didn't have a stand, it hits very hard, very deeply, very basically, sexual betrayal does, strikes at the manroot, at the very integrity of a man's self. Aah! There, the first thought of her, of Jenny, for today, no day goes by but that I think of her in some way or another, even though it's four and a half years since, now, four and a half long years of my selfmade hell, though what the hell is hell, it's another of those meaningless words like sin or evil or god. Nor am I out of it.

But just displace her image with the nearest thing, as usual, the nearest thing, long practice over four and a half years makes adequate.

When you drum on the bottom sheet with your tensely arched finger it booms hollow, amplified, to your ear pressed against the pillow. Cavity mattress, resonance, reverberation: drum delicate and interesting rhythms made complex by time-interval, due to the irregular cavity, weight disposition, the interstices between the whatnots,

Johnson, ah, cavity-walls, two skins of brick, rubble-filled, ties.

Today I can spend at my board, working, how marvellous, a whole day free to work, to do real work, my work, real work, vocation. I can put in a really hard day on the arts centre design. Ought really to go in for more competitions. It's the only way to become known, to break out of this destructive teaching, but I'm too lazy: perhaps too afraid, as well, too afraid of failing, of not . . .

. . . but the real satisfaction, even with success, whatever that means, would be in the work itself, as it is now, the real satisfaction, in the work. When I've done something, hewn it from my mind, then when it's actually built does not seem to matter, really, it's an accident, a commercial or economic accident, quite beyond my control.

But first enjoy lying here—what time? twenty past nine —lying this free morning, courtesy of the H.G., all morning if I like, to think as I choose, all the time in the world, time to use, misuse, abuse, self-abuse, time. Time. The great . . . wouldn't it be . . . yes, if you became dissatisfied with time, you'd go mad. Think—yes—if you wanted to catch the 9.31 and the 7.15 trains at the same time, that nothing could satisfy you but doing just that—yes, mad, they'd call you mad, that would be thought to be madness. But quite understandable. Like that old woman last week in Woolworths who asked some teenagers what day it was, and they just laughed at her, they must have thought she was mad, but she was asking, in all seriousness, what day it was, that day, so I told her, yes, it was Sunday, I thought. I was more sure at the time, now I forget what day it was: it might have been Monday, it rhymes with Sunday, I always have been prone to confuse things which rhyme, it's my nature. I choose not to change it. But today I forget what day it was, then, when the old woman had forgotten what day it was: I forget now, she forgot then, the same day, too, and what's the essential difference? Is she mad, was she mad, am I mad now, for forgetting, mad for telling her then, it was Sunday, I thought, on such scanty evidence, and subject to my known proneness? I just think the kids were stupid.

At least she was human in asking help of other humans: sometimes I think Marlene doesn't need other human beings at all. She needs something from me, though. But it's one of those . . . oh, christ, the bloody mess Marlene and that lot made last night still has to be cleared up. Don't want even to look. Still, soon I'll have the strength to get up, ha. Ooooh, last night, teachers are just, mistake to ask them round, I'm just not one of them, nor they one of me.

What do they do on their holidays, other teachers? What are they doing this morning, what's Marlene doing this morning? What's anyone doing this morning, for that matter? There are all these people, out there, in London, say, millions of them, this morning, all doing things, doing things—and I resent them doing things, for mine is the only way to live, mine are the only things worth doing, my doingthings.

Marlene is sleeping, I'm sure, she must have been late home. What a cow she is, staying after the others to make it look as though she was sleeping with me, and then not having any. But she didn't reckon on the last tube. I will not be stuffed in lifts! she says. Where will you be stuffed then, love? I says. Must tell Terry that. But a cow: I don't mind anyone suspecting I have women here, but it must be with absolute cause. Ah, why do I lust after Marlene? This is our Miss Crossthwaite, P.E. mistress, comes from

Yorkshire, y'know. It's her big tits, her lovely big tits, that's what I lust after, in the first place, anyway, oh let me rest my weary hands on your lovely big tits, Miss Crossthwaite, P.E. mistress, ours from Yorkshire, y'know.

Scott is a big tit, too, a big tit, though I've no wish to rest anything on him. I buy pop records, he says, for sociological reasons. And I listen to them because I like them, I says. Shocking, I think they found that, slightly. But they do too, really, only they won't admit it. Fascinating sociological study—balls! A load of old balls.

And Davison, too, the free liver. And I'm a floating kidney.

How do I get myself into these situations? Lust for the Marlenes of this world. Don't feed 'er, Mrs. Crossthwaite, you're overdoing it. And after last night lust isn't worth it. I shall continue to admire, my dear Miss Crossthwaite, your astonishingly big tits, but from well out of armsreach, the while frustrating myself with phantasies.

I hate these women who only want bits of me. I offer her the enormous totality of me, and she says, yes, I'll have the conversation bit, and the company bit, but not the bed bit, nor even the handsonmybigtits bit. I hate the partial livers. I'm an allornothinger. And it's usually nothing. Still. I shall allow her to spend her half-term on her own. So, have at thee with my codpiece, and farewell, Miss Crossthwaite of the monumental mammaries, other hands shall know thee, never these.

That's the thing with me, my thing with them, my way with women, I can always remove myself from them, absent myself, and stay away. Very good at it. When they won't be to me what I want them to be, then I am nothing to them. No crawling back, no being drawn, even if infatuated, fascinated by them. It's the one weapon I'm

proud to have, almost the only one I do have, the ability
to absent myself, and to stay absented: the ultimate in
weapons.

Oh, I know very well the way to have is by the way of
ignoring: but I want nothing of this deceit. By the way
of waiting and allowing and showing: but I want nothing
of these mortgages on the future.

Why don't you get up, you lazy sod? Today's the day
you've been longing for, today you can work at your board,
the one thing you really want to do, the one thing you
really can do. Right then: arise and change. To live is to
change. Put some jazz on. To wake up to. And then crap.

Where did all that lot come from? I didn't eat that much.
unearned excrement, that's what it is. But perhaps it
was all those compressed sawdust savouries that Marlene
brought. At enormous expense and loss of life. Yes, I must
have been champing away at those as sort of compensa-
tion, as a sort of substitute. Joseph's turn to buy the toilet-
roll: only one eighth of an inch left (plus or minus point
one) on the cylinder. Today—ah—I need not shave. I shall
not shave. Nor need I wash. I shall not wash. I shall do or
not do just as I like. Within my terms.

Jazz was, when I think of it, the first understanding I
had of what art meant, what it was all about. Those in-
credibly subtle voices from the worn surfaces—Bessie and
Ma and Ida—such dedicated sounds, the blues, poetry,
feeling expressed which coincided so completely with what
I was feeling or needed to feel. Used to play them over so
many times, when I was living at home. I suppose it subjects an art form to a special condition, repeating it so
many times, so that ever since I have been able to re-create
many of the sounds in my head, as I chose. And even the
special quality of the recordings—archaic and limited in

range—which added distancing, special, mine, mysterious. Joe Oliver was always the greatest for me, King Joe, some thought Louis, but I was always a King Oliver man, and no one could touch him, for sure, with a mute, he could make that cornet talk almost, with a mute, and you always felt he was a leader of an ensemble, not a soloist with sidemen, riding, relaxed, yet still driving, leading. Yes, the first understanding of what it was all about.

This kitchen needs cleaning. I'll do it later on. If I feel like it. I shall have nothing but coffee for breakfast—a big jug, real coffee, my only luxury, water, water, boil quickly. Can hardly smell the coffee. Must be affected by their smoking last night—open windows as soon as. Texture of irregular grains, rich foaming brown immediately after water poured on. Now I can smell it. Makes me feel hungry. Have a piece of cheese then. Stirred brown, milk-white hot, table by my board, my workplace, shrine, altar, do me a favour.

Firstfloor arches, the poor stucco imitation of channelled jointing, the semicircular fanlights, the thin cills: all this is now so firmly impressed upon my mind, upon my consciousness, that I wonder if I can ever design anything uninfluenced by it. The outline against the sky is now so moving, endearing to me. It has such rightness, even when it is not trying to be right, or there are things like economics against its being right, such grace, taste, good manners. All clichés about Georgian. But right, so right.

Of course, I would really like to be designing a Gothic cathedral, all crockets and finials and flying buttresses, but I must be of my time, ahead of my time, rather, using the materials of my time, the unacknowledged legislators, and so on, in accord with, of, my age, my time, my generation, my life.

But now: an arts centre for a town of half a million. The theatre should be fairly small, seating say five to seven hundred, yet the stage must be capable of mounting large-scale productions of opera and ballet—besides intimate chamber plays of the Strindbergian type. One solution is to use movable proscenium wings, together with a boom which can be raised or lowered, so that the pros. opening can be varied over a wide range. But when it's used in the smaller sizes then there is a vast booming stage area behind it which requires special acoustic treatment. Still, I don't think there's anything else I can do, so must assume this for the moment. Unless there was some cunning way of enabling the whole building to be reassembled for a particular type of stage—theatre-in-the-round, apron stage, opera, straight C19th picture frame—yes. But how? First of all, the weights to be moved would be so great as to involve machinery, definitely, too great for manual labour. And that means great cost, too. Still, expense is no object in Albert designs. So, if I had non-loadbearing party walls which could be moved through various angles to enclose a variable space—yes—and banked seat units which could also be grouped to suit each of several shapes. And a ceiling which could be raised or lowered. Yes. So how many shapes would I need? Large auditorium with proscenium, smaller intimate theatre, theatre-in-the-round, apron: four at least. The excess seat units would present a storage problem when the smaller auditoria were being used. The in-the-round would be the most awkward to arrange: it means cutting off the area of the pros. used in the other forms, except for an actors' entrance. And how adapt the ceiling to suit the differing forms? Ah, that's . . .

My father made this board for me, and a nice job he made of it, too. He's a clever old stick, my mother said, when she saw it. They're all right, my parents, I get on so much better with them since I've lived up here, not living there, seeing them only once a week, feel quite warm towards them.

Ah . . . I wonder what he expects, if he expects, to find in it? Gives opportunities to study derelicts, this rubbish-bin. Too high on lamp-post to see into, so he has to reach and dip. Newspaper. That's all today. Sorry mate. At least you read.

Bloody zip on my fly wants mending. Has done for weeks. Can do it today, don't hesitate, you can do it now. Ah my dear Miss Crossthwaite, if you feel domestic tonight come and mend my flies. Yes, think about this ceiling as I do it, it's all work, even if I'm not at the board.

Needles, cotton, odds in the handibag my mother gave me when I came up, to do for myself. Notch back the grey. Thread it in one—yes—in one. Rather shall a needle thread the small postern of a camel's eye.

Sun; could sit here longer; ceiling. The raising and lowering could be done easily enough hydraulically, but it's the shape that's difficult.

There: done it, slides most commodiously. Take care, Miss Crossthwaite, your calculated refusal to repair the breach has not resulted in its being long unmanned—beware a sudden zipping sound—for then I shall be undone! And you, foul Scott, I am now no longer incapacitated should I wish to confound the readings of your Meteorological Observation Club by peeing in the rainfall gauge!

Back to my board, refitted, refurbished. What about this bloody ceiling? Hasn't anyone else faced a problem like this? Look at books—yes—Mies, Corbu, Bannister bloody Fletcher, Frankl, Nervi, FLW, Pevsner, Knowledge a Young Woman should Have, Malory, Beckett, O'Brien,

Sterne—oh, what the hell. My problems are my problems: face alone, any others can offer only marginal comfort, relief.

Ah, aah! She's a . . . distraction. She's just the sort who can make me forget that women are cows, that women are, —fair, slimlegged, in blue; to me overwhelmingly . . . She walks well, round the Circus, my laterally-pitched Circus, walks so well on my Circus's eccentric pavements. Ah. Snares, delusions, frauds, women: all to propagate the breed, to perpetuate the . . . Not that the species has any real idea where it's going. Women are blindly beckoning, blindly propagating. Their loving words a fraud to make us, me . . . But loving nonetheless, and no fraud once revealed.

Ceiling. Just a blank. Look, Albert, mate, you're not going to work well this morning. Go out and have a drink. You'll feel guilty. But it's no good just sitting here facing the problem. Go away, forget about it, and it'll come to you, solve itself. Yes. As it has before. Yes.

Just after twelve. Right. Take dollybag, go shopping up Chapel Market, up Chap, good excuse, reason, rather.

Out, up, round into Amwell, Claremont, Penton: The Belvedere, Pentonville Tyre Service, *ΚΥΠΡΙΑΚΟ ΠΑΝΤΟΠΩΛΕΙΟ "Η ΚΕΡΥΝΕΙΑ"* Kyrenia Stores, John and Kay Fashions, Jak's Sea Bar, Leon's, The New Bright Restaurant.

The Queen's Arms. Didn't I see you in the Queen's Arms last night? That wasn't the Queen, that was my wife.

The laundry. My collars starched for school, oh yes, as I must at least not appear to be the delinquent teacher I am: carry anything off with a starched collar.

Chapel Market, Chap.

Carpets, keys cut, crockery, crowds not too bad today,

cheap, cheap. Aeromodels—remember making them myself: they never used to fly, and somehow this taught me to expect disappointment, very valuable.

And always in a crowd like this I am searching faces, all the time I am looking for Jenny, consciously or unconsciously, market faces, in tubetrains, in the crowds on television over at my parents, I look down the cast lists, too, of programmes because she once said she might take up acting seriously, and she could have done.

Stupid, this looking, stupid, this preoccupation with her and anything connected with her, or even things I arbitrarily connect with her, stupid, yes, but that's no answer, that's not the point, that's not removing the why, any of the whys. Why do I feel as I do in spite of agreeing it's stupid, why did I ever make such an issue about being an architect, about my career, vocation, that she must have resented taking second place to it? That must have helped to ruin it, to destroy it, our love, and she must have wondered why if I was so keen I just didn't go and do it. But it's not like that at all, not as easy as that, at all, it's . . . stop thinking.

A meat ticket pin. Pick up. Not so compulsive as with paperclips, of paperclips I am a compulsive pickerup. The question then arises, am I to consider myself bound to give a good home to every piece of wire left fortuitously (or so it seems) lying around? Already I admit market meat ticket pins, their shape pleases me, yet not hairpins, a dead end, hairpins, oh, the deadness, yes, the deadness of that sort of end has long been apparent to me, long since, of hairpins. But paperclips, now, yes.

Pop from the record stall, she never plays anything through to the end, constant musical titillation, she ought to be done for aural soliciting.

Please take a basket. I'll have that blonde dolly over there, I don't care if her parents weren't married, wrap her up. Rather have a trolley any day, it panders to my suppressed father instincts, even though I do only want to buy six eggs and some frankfurters. Whip round then, fast, rearwheel steering, drunk in charge of a supermarket trolley, three months and licence endorsed for running into old lady at coldmeat counter. Hit and run, out, out, 4/7d., here then, fivepence change and so farewell to the scene of the crime, the superdupermarket, out into the real Market.

Fruit, oranges, lots of veg., no strawberries yet, or peaches, then they come in with a wallop and you get sick of them, so many.

The Chapel House, good beer, comic tile murals in passage, Death of Cleopatra, Antony and Cleopatra, Act V, Sc. II, the muse of Music, smearedflesh children playing fairly underneath, waiting for their parents drinking inside.

The pub with the flowers, pots and pots on the tables, flowers, the Red House some call it, because of its long name, The Agricultural, which was too long for semiliterates to cope with, so they called it the Red House, the guvnor says, because of the facing brick, which is fairly unusual in a predominance of stocks.

A good guvnor, he is, one cannot choose too carefully the guvnor of one's pub.

Anyone I know here? Yes, several by sight, one by name, that's how it is. Ah, you know you're a regular when they pull your usual without your having to ask.

THANKS, SID.

A pro in the public, at lunchtime, too. I thought they would sleep all day. A bourgeois concept, no doubt.

Perhaps she's on days this week. Teeth like child's milk teeth, small, parallel edges, gap in middle. Is it possible to retain milkteeth undeveloped? No good you smiling at me, anyway, dolly, I'm not a potential customer. Why aren't I?

Because Jenny was so good, so what I wanted, anyway, that I can't bring myself to, for money, nor can I love anyone else, either, so I can't get it that way. But Jenny wasn't that good, really, at making love, when I think about it, not subtle at all, keen on just getting it in. You can make love with eyes and touching fingertips, I said to her once, when I was very angry, and it hurt her, and she tried, after that, but only when she chose to, when she wasn't feeling aggressive towards me. I think we both had different ideas about making love, perhaps we all do, sex means very different things to each of us, what it's about. And always lovemaking with Jenny was dependent upon circumstance rather than desire, upon opportunity rather than need or whim. One afternoon, in the summer vac, we had been out playing tennis, near her house, and the others had left, and I had been wanting her all day, Jenny, so I held her suddenly and took her up to her bedroom, and made love to her quickly, seriously, almost violently, and I remember she was particularly firm and tight that day, and afterwards she said, Always make love like that, darling, always just like that. Which was not normally my way at all, liking as I do the formalities, the preliminaries, the tendernesses, the innocencies, but for her the impromptu made it good for her. Memorable for her?

———GOT A HORSE FOR THIS AFTERNOON, SID?

———I GOT A FILLY FOR WEDNESDAY NIGHT.

Ah—he knocked and nearly dropped it. Old as he is, he still knows how a glass will behave when pushed, gravity is a constant, he remembers still knowledge he learnt as a child, painfully learnt, that glasses break when they fall after being pushed off a table, this is the constant of experience.

Pity Georgie isn't here lunchtimes, for the piano. Great he is, so in control, found his way in this way, playing the songs of forty years ago with such dedication, interest, sheer interest. That's the thing about the Angel, all the pubs have something going on in them, singing and dancing, life, you need never feel alone, in one sense, compared with the insufferable suburbs like Worcester Park or Sutton, where the pubs are like mausoleums, museums with stuffed people and not a sound but the cash register and the slurping of gargle.

——BOTH HE AND HIS WIFE WERE MARRIED, Y'KNOW.

That forerib of beef looks marvellous. And the ham.

SID, I'LL HAVE A BEEF ROLL, PLEASE.

——ONION?

Do I want onion? Yes, lovely raw crisp onion, with lovely raw underdone forerib of beef.

YES PLEASE, SID. HEARD ANY GOOD STORIES LATELY?

——I'M ALWAYS HEARING GOOD STORIES. DID YOU HEAR ABOUT THE TRAMP WHO WAS WALKING ALONG OXFORD STREET AND FOUND A DUMMY WITH FIVE QUID IN IT, SO HE THOUGHT HE'D INVEST IT IN A BIT OF THE OTHER AND WENT TO THIS OLD SCRUBBER. SHE DIDN'T WANT TO KNOW UNTIL HE SHOWED HER THE LOOT, BUT THEN SHE TOLD HIM TO GO AND HAVE A BATH, SO HE DID, AND WHEN HE CAME BACK SHE SAW HE HADN'T WASHED HIS JOHN THOMAS, SO SHE SAID, YOU DIRTY OLD MAN, GO AND WASH IT, SO HE DID, AND WHEN HE CAME BACK SHE SAID, THAT'S BETTER, NOW HAVE YOU GOT THE LETTER? AND HE SAID, CHRIST, DO I HAVE TO HAVE REFERENCES FOR IT AS WELL?

YES, SID, YES!

Fairly funny, yes, I could work on it.

There should be thicker filling towards the centre to compensate for the thicker bread part; each roll should contain protein and fat to balance the carbohydrate, and it might also be considered useful to include some essential roughage, like onion in the present case; certainly there should be protein in every roll; no butter, but beef dripping, for the purist. A dissertation upon the roll. Upon the beef roll.

——YOU PULL IT, THEN. AGAIN.

——CUT IT.

——NO, IT'LL JUST GROW AGAIN.

——NO, IT'LL GROW AGAIN. PULL. PULL! DON'T MIND ABOUT HURTING ME, JUST PULL IT OUT.

That's just what life is like, when you're old, I suppose, suddenly a bloody great long hair will grow out of your face, just grow, for no reason, well I suppose not really just like that, but that's how you notice it, that's how it seems to happen.

——WHAT YOU HAVING, JOHN?

THAT'S NICE OF YOU. BITTER PLEASE.

My name's not John, but it'll do, it's okay, for a pub name, John. Yes. I could have a different name for each pub round here, or a different identity, and a different identity too. But I should always want to be known as an architect, to preserve this essential myself, my identity, my character.

——SEEN YOU DOWN CHAP REGULAR LIKE, AND IN HERE, TOO.

YES, I LIVE NEAR, DOWN PERCY CIRCUS.

——DO YOU, THEN? WANTS DOING UP, DUNNIT, BUT THEY'LL GET ROUND TO IT SOONER OR LATER, I SPOSE.

No use saying I enjoy it decadent and decaying, decrepit,

like my state, London's state, England's state, man's state, the human condition.

YES, I SUPPOSE THEY WILL. YOU HAVE A STALL, DON'T YOU?

Expertise of Sid, the way he slices lengthwise along french loaf, spreads marge on both halves.

——YES, FRUITSTALL.

Play the identities game? Who am I? What am I? I must be taken for nothing but an architect, to preserve myself. So not to play with him, he's the sort who'd end up by saying, I know what you are, mate, you're a bleeding stupid twat.

Another drink then, for us. Yes.

Another drink.

The customers are nearly all old, here, in this pub, predominantly the old are customers here.

Another, yet another drink, then.

You ought to get back and work. You know you'll feel guilty. Another drink, then, just one.

THREE ALREADY, THEN SID? YOU MUST BE JOKING!

Out into—it's full, of people, stalls, cabbage, boxes, purple packingpaper, bruised fruit—my Chap.

That brisket looks good. Buy some. Yes. Protein to do something to the beer.

QUARTER OF SCOTCH BRISKET, PLEASE.

Lovely, lean, can't wait to eat it. Go down by canal then, yes.

Across the High Street, down Duncan Street, Clerkenwell County Court, to Vincent Terrace: British Waterways Regent's Canal, London Anglers Association PRIVATE FISHERY. Coarse grass on fortyfive degree slope straight to edge. Oil on water. Tunnel entrance, through trees, no barges, sun, sun, how unexpectedly quiet here, kids fishing, railings, sun, brisket.

That's the trouble with being a teacher, you're always afraid someone's going to catch you doing something unteacherly. Didn't I see you in Vincent Terrace by the canal railings, eating a quarter of Scotch brisket? Do it surreptitiously, then, guiltily, quickly, bolt it. But it's great, all the same, succulent, yes, succulent is the word I was wanting.

Swan. The proud swan. Yet how do I know it is proud? I the observer place on it the quality of proudness myself. The swan itself may or may not feel proud: of having feathered three lady swans, for instance, or of having fathered fourteen cygnets over the years. But only the swan knows that. Everything is subjective.

Something nasty in that bush. That even I should understand. A mother superior writes.

Back down Colebrooke Row, then, must start working, work right through now until bed, to make up for it. A ceiling of variable shape and capable of being raised and lowered. Wonder who designed Sadler's Wells Theatre then? Thirties? Yes. His problem was fairly straightforward, large theatre for one kind of staging, I would have thought. As was his solution. Possibly an oddly-shaped site, though.

Every time I pass round the back of Sadler's Wells there's an awful café smell blasted out at noselevel. All operasingers live on when they are engaged here is toast and tea and stickybuns. That's what it smells like, anyway. To build them up. Perhaps that's what Miss Crossthwaite nourishes her bosom on, too, and savoury knickknacks, and when women like her reach her age then they start to smell, too, women's smell, which can be nasty, yes, from Miss Crossthwaite certainly, it puts one off, me off, for one. Women's smell. Perhaps I do, too, smell, or stink, there is no doubt a man's smell that puts women off. But I just think I don't, find it strange to think I could, just as I still find it strange to think of myself as a man, as a boy no longer, even at twenty-eight; as when some kid at school says That man, and I think Who? And then realise he means me, and am still surprised. As I am too when I make involuntary snufflings, noises through my mouth, or nose, or when I spit slightly in the middle of a sentence, and the kids notice, and some laugh, and I realise that as I am getting older I am less in control of my body, though more and more in control of my mind, and I fear, I fear for the future. But I am glad that I have had the chance to observe myself growing older, carefully, that I can do so, as I feel I should not have done had I married early, had become a husband with a proper job instead of wanting to . . .

The Shakespeare's Head. New pub. Old one fell down. Ten minutes after closing time one night, just as all the operalovers were wending their uplifted ways homeward, the front of the pub fell out. Just fell out into the road. Wallop. An act of god, they concluded, a most irresponsible sort of a god, evidently.

Myddelton Passage. And these uncomely flats. How the same company that owns Myddelton Square and Claremont Square could put up these, even a century and a quarter later, I just don't understand. Anyone who does less than his best, even unconsciously, must create guilt within himself, severer in proportion to the lesser-than-best that he has done. Whoever designed the rubbish at places like Sutton, Worcester Park and St. Helier, for instance, must bear, have borne, an enormous burden of guilt, probably quite unaware of its origin, of its cause.

Through the wide wicket, the space through which there is a Georgian prospect of St. Paul's. Myddelton

Square, with its prospect, and subtly-pitched dormers, and finely-beaded fanlights. To Claremont—no, to Amwell, Great Percy Street, and my Circus.

And they've cut what grass there was in the centre, and at the window I can smell it, fresh, glad I opened it before I left, the room full of the freshness of newcut summer grass.

I feel tired. Breathe deeply, good, yes, sleep for half an hour, then awake refreshed, work like hell, yes.

Pollard, The White Goddess, Mies, my books, aaah . . .

Hell! What time is it? Seven! You bloody fool! Guilt. Guilt.

Close the window. Specks of smut on my drawing, hell, London smut. Smuts. Still.

Another day just frittered, as far as ever, farther because nearer death, from success, whatever that is, whatever that may mean, frittered, the worst crime, against myself, guilt.

Smuts, flecks of soot, coal. Damn. Won't clean off, ruined drawing, not that there was much to ruin, three lines of a . . .

Three lines. It's not nothing, exactly. Not exactly nothing.

Perhaps Terry will call this evening. Then that will take care of another day, send another lousy frittered day about its miserable business. Yes, I'll phone him, in a minute, yes.

Yes.

Guilt.

Three lines. . . .

*   *   *   *   *

*   *   *   *   *

The weding of our beloved Mr Alburt he was going to get marred to miss Croswait on the night befor he got parerlatick drunk to buck up inogth corag to say Yes. On the day they got marred he was sick twic

On thire honemoon they went to south End they had a lovly time at south End he spent a lote of money he spent about 6 penc

They had a bundol and got dievorsed

The death of Mr Albert He died of Bulgarian flue He was walking along and tript over his long bloand Hair.

We smash the school up because the teachers are not stricht and revolting it should be more stricht and we should be compeled to wire uniform insted of comeing a school in X Army Jackets and Jeans and X Army Boots and lever Jackets

The teachers are not stricht they let you do what you like Mr Alburt is one of them

*   *   *   *   *

Albert picked up his cup, scraped its unglazed base on the thick white edge of the saucer, and drank tea. The tea had a trembling encrustation of tannin, and had been made with sterilised milk. Albert minded neither of these things, on this occasion; on other occasions he might well have minded, might even have entered upon a complaint to the management, but on this occasion he did not mind.

Heat was transmitted through the coarse china to burn the middle joint of his index finger; when this became un- bearable he put the cup down and gripped it again with bunched fingertips. What did they do before they put handles on cups, he thought. Who first thought of handles? Perhaps it was the Beaker Folk. Yes, let it be the Beaker Folk. One member of the Beaker Folk was constantly burning his stubby fingers on hot beakers of bedtime maresmilk, and always dropping and breaking them. Yes, thought Albert, and this would convincingly account for the enormous quantity of beaker fragments available to be excavated by archaeologists. Then one bedtime this otherwise simple, even obtuse, man (it could not have been a woman, Albert felt sure) had the concept of the Handle come upon him in a moment of high apocalyptic inspiration. The Handle. Perhaps he made the first one from a twig sprung into appropriate holes formed before the beaker was baked. Later, he had improved on this by pinching the beaker into a convenient shape. Then he had thought himself eminent enough to break away and found a tribal sub-dynasty of his own: the Pinched Beaker Folk.

Terry watched three Somalis at the next table. Small brown paper packets passed from hand to hand. The men looked normal enough, Terry thought, not at all like dope fiends as featured in *The People*. Perhaps they were only pedlars and not actual addicts. Drugtakers are the absolute example, he thought, of those who live only in the present, for the present, the only way to live: they see no farther than the next fix, they are willing to sacrifice everything for it, abandon all lien on the future whatsoever. Perhaps he should try drugs? To help him forget Janine? Drink was no use, it made him morose and it distended his stomach. But which drugs?

Two prostitutes sat talking and smoking at another table. ⌐Half-caste, straight hair, yellowing teeth, doglipped, long graceful hands, thin.⌐   ⌐Dyed daffodil-yellow hair, blenched skin, cast in left eye, short, odd effect of physical breaking-up.⌐

"I met this blind man on the bus coming home tonight," said Albert, quietly, to Terry. "He'd been waiting ten minutes for a 19, he said, and people in the queue kept on getting on other buses. He went on and on about them. Said you've got to be black today: you're better thought of. Blind prejudice if you like. Anyway, I told him when a 19 came and the conductor helped him on to the bus, but he still went on and on. 'Christmas Day and they're all over you,' he said, 'asking you all the time Are you sure you don't want to cross the road? The rest of the year they don't want to know.' Then he just sat there and whistled a fragment of a tune over and over again, as if to keep himself company."

"He ought to think himself lucky," said Terry, "that he's got such a good excuse to demand help of people, to demand their sympathy. If healthy people do it then they automatically get kicked in the balls."

Both Albert and Terry thought of Jenny and Janine, their respective betrayers, respective ballskickers, they, the betrayed, thought that this was the particular conflict in society in which they were inextricably involved: that there was now no reason for fidelity, that there had seemed to be one when they were young, but that there was now no reason, and they could not quite blame the women for

it; now the only reason for fidelity was itself, faith in a
concept, in a particular virtue which must of absolute
necessity be its own reward. Sin and evil they could understand the passing of, these were now mere archaisms,
words at best synonymous with wrong: but there was still
somewhere pure within them the concept of fidelity.

The blonde one reminded Terry, oh so very faintly, in
the way she held her head, of Janine.

"Let's go," he said.

Albert followed.

Between the highlevel Fenchurch Street line to the
north, and the tall bricked-window façades of the London
Western Dock warehouses to the south; cut horizontally
by Cable Street in the north and the Ratcliffe Highway in
the south; an area of two-storey Georgian cottages, savaged
by the war, slums before it, largely derelict now, all con-
demned, still awaiting razing. And centrally there is Wellclose Square, warehouses and tall second-ratings, lovely
of its nature, quiet and dark and serene in its decrepitude.
But in the centre there are a school, a playground, and a
house, that are excrescences, that are not fitting.

Albert kept close by the wall through Grace's Alley into
Wellclose Square. Two-thirds of the way down someone
had recently relieved himself against a blanked-off shop-
front. The flakeworn paving was marked like a delta, like
a chaotic candelabra, like a fistful of snakes. Albert paused,
fascinated, then turned his head to look at the patterns in
reverse. Never content to leave well alone, he unzipped
his fly and attempted to impose the pattern of art on
nature. Terry joined in, laughing, and made the whole
area into a sea, the paving awash over the patterns, ruin-
ing the subtle tracery under the lamp's light.

"Bastard! Bastard!" shouted Albert. The façades on

one side reflected the sound, the gaptoothed bombsite on the other sucked in the sound:

"Baa! Baa!" gave back the façades, more gently, and the gaptoothed bombsite took the echoes as greedily and as gratefully as it had taken the original sounds.

Albert moved quickly into Wellclose Square. Terry followed, laughing at Albert's anger. Albert was further offended by the clutter of buildings and wirenetting in the centre of the Square: seeing empty milkbottles on a doorstep, he picked one up, looked quickly around, and, seeing no one to rat, he threw it as hard as he could, overarm, as if it were a grenade, towards the playground. It burst with a deeply satisfying splintering sound. Terry tried to look as though he were not with Albert. Albert tried to look as though he were not with Terry, laughing delightedly.

In a Nigerian café a negro came to their table with an electric razor to sell.

"Two pun," he kept demanding. Albert could not think of two quickly enough to tell him. The shaver looked new. Albert decided he would buy it. Searching, he found five and ninepence. He borrowed a pound from Terry, and offered the total to the man. Albert did not care whether he accepted it or not; he had no more money, nor had Terry; it was up to the negro. He tried for five minutes to extract more, coming finally down to asking for a cup of tea, for this too to be refused. It was not that Albert, or that Terry, sought to deprive him of a cup of tea, but that they just had no more money with them on this occasion. Suddenly the negro gave in, picked up the twenty-five and ninepence, and went out through the hardboard-shuttered door.

Albert inspected his new acquisition. There was no indication that it worked, he realised: he should have tested it before buying it. He asked the man behind the counter whether he could plug it into a light socket, but was refused.

Albert put the shaver in its box, carefully, put it in his pocket, and spoke for some time:

"So I went back after the holiday, quite refreshed as I usually am, and my form were giggling about over bits of newspaper, two or three groups of them, and making it bloody obvious they wanted me to come and see what they were up to. So I didn't. Then when I began to call the register one of the girls brought out a clipping and put it on my desk without a word. 'Teaching at Tough School Contributes to Teacher's Suicide', it said, and it was only a report of my predecessor's suicide over Whitsun, Burroughs, Bunny they called him. I just took no notice—after all, I didn't know him, did I, and if they thought they could break me, then they'd misjudged me. Gas, it was, just turned on the gasring in his digs and sat in the armchair. I just went on calling the register, but later the Head sent for me, and asked me if I'd stay until the end of the term. Don't worry about Burroughs, he said to me, he had many reasons for suicide outside school. Yes, I thought, and he had forty-three inside school, as well, and they're kicking up hell in my classroom at this moment. I can't stand this Head: he's so bloody weak, and he doesn't back up his teachers. In my first week I took a boy to him who'd been grossly impertinent to me, and when I'd told him of this he turned to the boy and said, Now let's hear your side of it. I ask you! And when he's talking to you he looks at a spot midway between your chin and your collar, never in your eyes."

"So you're going to leave?" Terry asked.

"No, it looks as if I'm stuck there until the end of term

anyway. Just the way he put it made me pretty sure he'd fix it with the Office."

"The bastard."

"The kids seem half scared by Burroughs' suicide, and yet pleased. They really hated him, I know. Yesterday, this was, and at the end of school one of them came up to me, Sweetman his name is, and said, We're going to have a meeting tonight to decide about you. And this morning, as soon as he saw me, he said, We've decided, and we're all chipping in for a gasring for you. They're half-serious, too, that's what's so interesting, half-serious. And then there was this kid Weir, who was never in class. I used to call the register, and his name was last, 'Jackie Weir', and the class at first used to chorus, 'He's not here', and then when they'd got to know me after a couple of days, it was 'Jackie Weir—He's a queer', mingled with the 'He's not here'. And the Head this morning tells me to take him off roll: he is indeed queer, and has been picked up flogging it around the more classy W.1 conveniences, and sent to an approved school—to finish his education, of course. The girls are at least normal: there's one who waits behind purposely so that I shall watch her wiggle her sweet little bum at me as she goes out of the door. I've been warned to watch the girls in the afternoons: some of them are apparently in the habit of coming to school, getting their marks, and then going off to tea-dances up west. Girls are always being brought back by attendance officers. There's this sort of uneasy balance, with the boys as well, between the police outside school and the teachers within. They know they're less likely to get into real trouble inside school, yet it's so boring for them, so bloody boring. And that's a failure in the teaching, of course: but the situation at this school is so extreme that any teacher coming into it from outside is beaten before he starts. You can see the staff are beaten, from the look in their eyes, from the way they go about the corridors. And I'm beaten, too, at this school. When I came up here I used to think I was at least a fairly competent teacher, even if I was certainly not a dedicated or inspired one. But the frightening thing here is that any sort of punishment has failed as a deterrent: whatever you do to them doesn't stop them doing what they want to, again and again. I hit them on the head with my knuckles as much to relieve my feelings as to try to stop them shouting or to make them pay attention. And they know all the rules—that you're not supposed to hit them on the head, or hit them at all if you're on supply, for that matter, and that they're not to be kept in for more than half an hour. I know that the standard answer is to treat them with lovingkindness, but you try it, mate, I've not got that much lovingkindness. And they'd think you soft. The Assistant Head—a right Amazon of a woman who doesn't seem aware of about eighty percent of what goes on in the school—said the kids would listen and behave if my lessons were sufficiently interesting. I told her that since they'd been interesting enough for every class I'd ever taken before, it might just possibly be the general standard of this particular school that was at fault. I was beaten before I ever got there. The timetable she worked out for me doesn't help any, either: about half of it is English, but I also do music, a couple of maths lessons, games on Wednesdays and several general periods which I naturally use for architecture or geology."

But Albert paused! A tap dripped in the sink behind the counter. Albert thought with awe of the vast resources behind that tap: the miles of pipes, of mains, the reservoirs, the rivers, the rain. He imagined with what wonder an African immigrant must regard the water supply: "It comes in pipes, you just have to turn a tap thing, man. And that same water is the same as the Queen drinks. When I turn that tap thing, man, I'm connected with the same water she uses. And the sewers, man, they connect, too, she don't use no special sewer, they all connect up and side by side hers and mine come out at Barking Creek. That's a democratic country for you, man."

⇥Eyes the brown of dead bracken, lips of similar thickness threequarters of their length, dyedblack hair, glinting skin.↵ Up the stairs. A negro padlocked the door behind her. But Albert continued!

"I told you the sods pinched my pen a couple of weeks ago? I was reading this novel recently about a teacher in the east end who won over the kids by love and kindness, morality and honesty, against tremendous odds—talk about sentiment and wish-fulfilment! I can just see my lot coming to me at the end of term with a present—or even my pen back—addressed to sir, with their love! These things just don't mean anything to these kids in this school: that's what's so frightening, and I've not been frightened in a school before. Not frightened by their violence, though that's bad enough, but just by these unknown forces of character. These kids will just go on knocking off my pens for as long as I have pens to knock off. I'm sure that even if I chained a pen to the desk then next day they'd bring a pair of stillsons and have it away."

"Did you tell the Head?" Terry asked.

"Of course, but he seemed to think I was stupid for leaving things around anyway. Always lock things up, Mr. Albert, he said. He's always smiling, in a sort of slitfaced way, the Head: I'm sure he'd have that same smile on his face as he eased a knife into your back, quite sure. And I'll tell you a funny thing: the men's bog is opposite his room, across a lightwell, and there's this long window which whenever I go in there is open a few inches just at fly-level. But it may be the women—theirs is just opposite, too, for that matter. Nearly all of them are married but look frustrated—no, not frustrated, exactly, but as though their husbands had been neglecting the foreplay. But of course I was stupid to leave my pen lying there: it won't happen again. Here, today I was playing them some Carl Orff in a music lesson—a record of his setting of Catullus, good, simple, thumping stuff, and when we got to the phrase 'Da mi basia' repeated several times with increasing passion, this little Greek Cypriot girl suddenly sat up, said 'Oh!' and smiled all over her face. I suppose the Latin is similar to the Greek; so at least I pleased one of them that day, though god knows if she understood any of the rest. She's quite a nice little girl, actually, long black hair—how real black hair shows up against dyedblack—and skin like Pentelic marble. But there's a Greek Cyp bastard called Erotokritou who whenever he sees me, several times a day often, comes up to me and says, 'Have you bin sayin' fings about ma famly?' Sometimes he says 'What you bin sayin' about ma famly?' Or 'You bin sayin' fings about ma famly!' For no reason. And he's violent, he has this reaction of violence to practically every situation. I've watched him with other kids in the playground, and he—not exactly scares me, but disturbs me, makes me uneasy, apprehensive. There is latent aggression in everything he does, in every movement he makes. He's a member of the Corps, too, which is a gang of about five who wear ex-army boots and who drill each break in the playground. They're quite disciplined in their way, and they terrorise the other kids. The Head ought to insist that they come to school in ordinary shoes, of course, but I don't think he's even interested. The Corps practises kicking-in in unison—my god! Unless you came to this school you just wouldn't believe half the things that go on. You'd hardly see it as a school at all as you know schools: there's no set of rules, or even habits, to which the kids will conform or that they will even acknowledge. I've never been anywhere before, for instance, where they do not even accept that they must not talk in class: when I shut them up they resent it as though I am curtailing an inalienable freedom. And I see their point, in a way, too. But no one can teach under such conditions. You have to establish your own set of rules, let alone your own obedience of those rules, your own discipline. Which takes all the time, and an incredible amount of nervous energy. It's like I'm working at the frontier of civilisation all the time."

Albert went over to the jukebox and put a shilling in it. He spent a long time choosing three records: he found two he wanted to hear, and set the ingenious mechanism working to bring this about, but the third choice was not easy. Eventually he just pressed the button corresponding to his favourite number, twenty-nine, and then returned to sit with Terry. The two women looked at him contemptuously as soon as they heard his first record begin.

"Some classes have so many Cypriots in them that the register reads like the *dramatis personæ* of a Greek tragedy," Albert offered. "They form a conclave within the school, too, eating at exclusively Cyp tables, in gangs, and in class one smart one will catch and understand what I say and pass it on to the others. Yet I can begin to sympathise with why the older ones are restless and unmanageable: in Cyprus at fourteen they'd be accepted as men, and be doing men's jobs."

Albert thought: a block of wood, a plank of wood. When does a block become a plank? When does a plank become a block? At what point do you see that a block has become a plank, at what stage a plank a block? Plank. Block. He thought about them until the words became meaningless to him, then ludicrous to him, then nothing to him. And he was left with wood. Wood is wood is wood, he said to himself, pleased.

"If we go on half-educating these kids any more," he said suddenly to Terry, "then the violence will out. I'm sure they know they're being cheated, that they're being treated as subhuman beings. And the school *is* a microcosm of society as a whole."

There was this tremendous need for man to impose a pattern on life, Albert thought, to turn wood into planks or blocks or whatever. Inanimate life is always moving towards disintegration, towards chaos, and man is moving in the opposite direction, towards the imposition of order: as the animals are, too, but to a far lesser extent. This was the paradox: for the fundamental rhythm of life was the alternating disintegration-reintegration of matter. Perhaps five hundred million years ago matter became capable of maintaining itself by reactions to stimuli: that is to say, it became life.

The past of a man's life could always be controlled in this way, be seen to have a fixed order because it was passed, had passed: almost always, that is, for when it could not be controlled then madness was not far away. When something was passed, it was fixed, one could come to terms with it; always the process of imposing the pattern, of holding back the chaos. Like antiques, collecting them, a manifestation of the security of a pattern, harking back to the safeness of things passed. His father, he had seen, often preferred the less good, if known, to the possibly better, if unknown: and Albert felt himself always to be liable to do the same and consciously fought against it, trying to see everything freshly, trying to realise in practice his theoretically absolute freedom of will, freedom from the passed. In most things he succeeded: but for Jenny, with the memory and grief of whom he had not come to terms, upon which he had not imposed a pattern.

As an example, too: Albert walking from Balls Pond Road into Mildmay Park, buying a peach on the way, the third time realising he had done the same thing twice before, who was free to buy grapes, or an orange, or an apple, and to wander along Newington Green Road, for one alternative, had imposed a pattern unconsciously, in such a simple matter, had formed a habit, shoring what up against what decay, against what chaos?

"But what if he were to do me in?" enquired one of the women, more loudly than she had been speaking before. Albert remarked upon and commended, to himself, her pretty employment of the Subjunctive: in this tense's struggle with the Indicative in the constant levelling tendencies of language, this usage by this woman, whatever her moral standards, was indeed encouraging, a blow struck back for precision and subtlety.

Terry thought that that was one of the things that hurt most about Janine leaving him, the being forced back into this sort of world, this seeking company in pubs and cafés, without the special warmth and kindness of the company of a woman. That was perhaps the best reason he had to hate her, for withdrawing these things from him, and somehow making it impossible at the same time for him to ask them of any other woman. It had destroyed the confidence he needed to ask them of any other woman. That hurt, as well as the other things. And she made him feel like a youth again, immature: he remembered her saying to him that the ability to make painful but firm decisions was one of the chief signs of maturity. Which was why he was here, in a Cable Street café, acting immaturely, listening to music he despised and to conversation which bored him.

Albert thought of others' solutions to the sexual problem: the for-instance heavily-beringed women of about thirty-five to be seen in many Angel pubs: a half-inch of wedding and engagement rings on their finger, a sign of pride, of aggressive non-availability. Yet they must see sex as in many ways condemning them to drudgery through children, and dread it because of this. He needed someone who realised instinctively about the necessity of the illusion of love: which had taken him so long even to begin to understand. And the boy of fourteen who had talked more sense to him about sex than ever he had been able to command himself, and who accepted, accepted reversals in the same spirit if not with the same pleasure as conquests.

Albert stood up.

"I'm feeling in the mood for horrors," he said. "Let's drive round Worcester Park and St. Helier."

Terry stood up in agreement; he did not mind where they drove.

They walked through North East Passage into Well-close Square, kicking an empty beercan with considerable satisfaction, passing and re-passing to one another. In the Square an old man came out of one of the houses.

"Why don't you make more noise?" he suggested, without irony in his voice. "Just like a couple of kids."

The rebuke was so mild that Albert laughed with relief.

"We are just a couple of kids," he said.

They walked away from the Fiat, to avoid identifying it with themselves, once round the Square, and then came back to it.

"The theatre," said Terry, "is dead. Dead."

"I could give you a building that would make it live again," said Albert.

"It's nothing to do with buildings, that the theatre is dead, but because of the audience. You won't get good, living theatre until you get an audience with good and valid reasons for going, for being an audience."

Along the Ratcliffe, through the Rotherhithe, Bermondsey, Camberwell, Streatham: the bye-law streets and tunnel-back dwellings of nineteenth-century housing legislation: Mitcham: Morden: Sutton:

Deliberately, Albert caused Terry's random direction-taking to bring them past the house of Jenny's parents. Deliberately, too, he did not tell Terry.

Albert's full contempt was reserved for Worcester Park: St. Helier was bad but unpretentious, but Worcester Park was both very bad and pretentious at the same time. Street upon street of semi-detached mock-timbered gables, Norman arches on the porches, Gothic windows in the halls, bakelite door furniture throughout, intensely unimaginative front garden layouts, identical wroughtiron gates, twee lanterns to light the porches. William Morris was responsible for having started the movement which led to all this, Albert thought, but surely he could not have approved of Worcester Park?

Albert felt something large and hard in his pocket: it was the electric shaver. An idea came to him, and he asked Terry to stop outside the next house with a porchlight on. He opened the door and went through the gate up a shingle path. In the porch he carefully removed the bulb from the mock-renascence lantern with his fingers wrapped in a handkerchief, placed it in his pocket, and replaced it with the adaptor of the shaver. The shaver began to throb in his hand at once and he started to shave: it worked well, and he was particularly pleased with the way it cleaned the hard stubble above his top lip.

The hall light went on, the door opened, and a little fat man stood on the step. He had pulled on a dressing-gown over his pyjamas, but it was open at the fly to disclose a shadow of pubic hair.

"What the hell d'you think you're doing?" he demanded.

"Shaving," said Albert, not to be outdone.

The man reached inside the door and switched off the porchlight supply. Albert heard the telephone ping at the same time, and assumed someone was ringing for the police. Quickly he unplugged the shaver and, thrusting it into his pocket, he walked away down the path. The man followed: Albert realised he might take the Fiat's number if he reached the gate, so he turned and shouted melodramatically:

"I'm a desperate man, and I'll shoot if you come any nearer!"

The man laughed briefly, nastily and disbelievingly, and still came on. Albert took the bulb from his pocket and quietly dropped it behind him. It burst with a noise similar to a pistol shot. The man turned and Albert heard the door slam behind him.

"Heigho for Georgiou's, I think, mate," he said to Terry. "When I was a kid we used to call that poshing lightbulbs, poshing, poshing, it's a fine word."

* * * * *

Proposition: That These Children's Speech is Bad.
For the Proposition: Miss Crossthwaite.
Against the Proposition: Mr. Albert.

✂ *Miss Crossthwaite* said that they all knew the speech of children at this school to be bad: every time one of them opened his or her mouth to speak the result was almost invariably hideous, an offence to the ears. Their speech was slovenly, like their personal habits.

✂ *Mr. Albert* said that 'bad', 'hideous', and 'slovenly', were not words that could be meaningfully used about speech: a child saying *prize* for *praise* was using the same sound as in the word *prize*. The sound itself was not 'wrong', therefore, but its context was not that of so-called standard speech: accurately, it was only in a social context that sounds could be described as misplaced. Often the different sound produced by these children required more phonetic effort to produce (for example, the glottal stop) than the one it replaced: how then could such speech be described as 'slovenly'? The offence to Miss Crossthwaite's lovely ears, Mr. Albert suggested, came about because these children were not speaking as she spoke herself, these children were not imposing the same pattern on their worlds as she imposed on hers: for who approves, Mr. Albert quoted Petronius without attribution, of conduct unlike his own? For communication within their own social context, the speech of these children was perfectly suited. As a teacher, he would point out to children that if they chose to move into other social contexts then they would probably not find acceptance unless they conformed to the speech conventions of the new one, accent being generally the easiest way of determining class origin: but he would never attempt to 'correct' children's speech provided they were making themselves clear to him; that is, provided they did not speak indistinctly.

✗*Miss Crossthwaite* was nevertheless convinced that she would still object when any child said 'ain't' in her hearing.

✗*Mr. Albert* said that while in his childhood 'ain't' was common, this usage had now shifted to 'ent' in London. This was an example of the continual progression of sound changes in speech, in the face of which any standardisation was quite wasted, even ludicrous. And the working-class always led in such speech changes, and the upper classes were farthest behind: the Queen, for instance, always *lanches* a ship, and uses *lorst* for *lost*.

✗*Miss Crossthwaite* said that the speech of the children of this school was bad and slovenly.

The bell went before a vote could be taken.

* * * * *

An Eye for Place

Of places most of all remembering comes.

Of Hungerford Lane that first tense evening,
for instance, where shadows, stacks and iron

escapes above us segmented the night
in a parody of a clerestory;
where I refrained in the obvious place,
choosing anti-romantically to wait
until we had reached the high limewashed vault
of the bridge; and where, while the savage trains
gunned behind their netting cage, I kissed you.

And this from one who always found more
in places than in people to love before.

My masculine room suddenly made a home
by the careful discard of un-needed clothes;
my austere room tender with your warmth,
made holy by the ritual of our loving;
its certain books you held gaining almost
the character of relics with your leaving;
and the sweet residual reminder of its bed
as I entered it again at night alone.

London that summer seemed full of tall cranes,
strutted and frail and busy in our way.

Your windhammered hair in the spring wind
on the breast of Nottingham Castle:
and the company of friends to whom we seemed
like lovers in a ballad:

the skewed house in which we stayed
for three sacred nights;
the room with its barely-yielding bed
and absurdly-patterned walls:

your chaste pain, although we must
have joined a hundred times
before, making you for this once
my pure and childlike virgin:

my terror of loss, as, dead in sleep,
you spurned my tenderness:
yet, waking, made sweet recompense
in reassurances:

And last, *The Trip to Jerusalem*,
another consummation:
a kind of voyage to a holy land
to help us understand.

And oh but how this sweet remembering numbs!

But most of all at
Balgy, where
the plump seatrout leapt
from our pool,
and ochre seashells
fell from rocks
tinkling when the tide
had left them:

You and I
by our fire leaning
against rock
rough as a catstongue,
while the moon
hung caught in a wire

fence on the
cliff above the stream:

And our free bathing
by the fault,
like pure animals
who never
knew and hated man,
to make *and why do I run my mind up*
and down the honed edge of memory so constantly hold
my brain to the while these shoes did not know her since
then I have worn out two and partially a third pair of
shoes....

*   *   *   *   *

Albert said: Joseph, mate, you're a native: what the hell
am I supposed to do with the kids round
here? I don't give a damn if they screw each
other without my knowing, but when they
drop frenchie packets in my wastepaper
basket in the middle of a lesson, what am I
supposed to do?

Joseph said: Ignore it.

Albert said: I blush, that's my trouble, I blush.

Joseph said: Don't kid me you lead the sheltered life, mate,
what with all these birds I see fluttering in
and out of here. Who was that one night
before last, for instance? She your regular
bird then?

Albert said: No, but she's someone else's. I mean, I
wouldn't have you think she was being

wasted, or anything. I'll tell you a funny story
about her, mate, though, at least, you'll think
it's funny. This is a dolly I had about three
years ago, very keen on her, I was, very keen
indeed. Then I pushed it too hard, as I always
do, it's a sort of defence, a sort of need to be
hurt so I push me luck—so didn't see her for
a couple of years, then something happened
that's never happened before—I sort of got
friendly with her again—only there was never
anything sexual about it—don't laugh—and I
could take her to parties and things and enjoy
myself—that is, not worry who the hell she
was talking to or who was trying to make her
—and this was all very fine, and I know the
bloke she's going to marry—she's getting married in three weeks—and I like him a lot, too.
So it's a nice clean friendship: but the night
before last she turns up shortly after I got
back from school—you know I'm bloody dead
when I get back and can't think for about an
hour. Anyway, I make her some tea and feed
her a biscuit and we natter and it's all very
domestic and she goes and washes her hair
and I say how domestic this is and isn't she
taking a bleeding liberty as though I was
Mike her bloody intended. And she says No,
she thinks she looks very sexy like this. At
which I can only laugh, in my way. Anyhow,
so when I can think I suggest we go to the
theatre, not just wanting to talk to her all the
evening, and knowing already there isn't a
chance of it going the way it should if she was

any other dolly, and she's dead unenthusiastic about going out at all. But only afterwards do I really notice this, and finally we go off to the bloody theatre, and d'you know what? She falls asleep—not once, but twice, once in each act. Now, I know the play was bleeding awful —the theatre's dead, mate, quite dead, you know, especially the intellectual theatre, but these bloody critics mislead you with their small change—but I ask you! But now, here at last I get to the point, last night she rings me up and asks me how I enjoyed the play. Not much, says I. Nor did I, says she, I wish we hadn't gone. What would you rather have done, then, I ask her. Stayed in and made love, she says. Jesus Christ! And she's getting married in three weeks, too!

Joseph said: Birds are like that.

Albert said: But you notice she didn't bloody say it when I could have done something about it—if she'd really wanted it, then she would have said so at the time, wouldn't she?

Joseph said: Not necessarily. Birds are like that.

Albert said: Honest, Joseph, I just can't justify women's ways to men. The lot of them beat me. Like these birds at school, that I was telling you about just now, before I got sidetracked. They come up to me after lunch—they seem to run a lunchtime brothel somewhere—and I can smell it, mate, smell it. They've just had it off somewhere. And they come and stand at my desk as close as possible, probably thinking I know nothing about it or something. Or seeing

if I do, and have got the guts to say something. It's enough to drive you round the twist.

Joseph said: Ignore it.

Albert said: That's the last thing I can do.

Joseph said: You got sexual problems, mate, sexual problems, that's your trouble.

Albert said: Of course I have, but not simple ones. It's
nothing like as simple as going out and screw-
ing some old scrubber for a few bob.

Joseph said: You make it difficult for yourself, mate. Why
isn't it as simple as that?

Albert said: It's all connected with Jenny, and therefore
with the whole of myself, everything I am.

Joseph said: You're just using her as an excuse. You could
forget these things easily enough if you didn't
bloody think so much about them. Look, they
either do or they don't. Otherwise you're on
your tod, mate, strictly on your tod.

Albert said: I think I had more, once.

Joseph said: Then you were bloody mistaken. You were
kidding yourself. All this soul-mate stuff you
mean?

Albert said: Something like that.

Joseph said: You were mistaken, then, and you're just off
your squiff if you think you'll ever have it
again.

Albert said: You see, in one way I'd just like to go up to
some bird round here, for a try, and say 'Give
with the reechy kisses, babe', just to see what
she'd say. Of course, I know what she'd say if
she was a workingclass character in a book—
'Cool!' or 'Get you' or 'Are you off your
chump?' But what would she actually say?

Joseph said: Get stuffed?

Albert said: Perhaps. I can only find out by trying it, of course. Here, you know what they did to one teacher today? One of the girls just took out her lighter in the middle of a lesson and set fire to the curtains. Killing, isn't it? I've had the curtains in my classroom taken down.

Joseph said: Kids today don't seem to have much imagination.

*   *   *   *   *

Justin, Erotokritou, Fleming, Sweetman, Mee. They drill most precisely. They have practised for hours. Single file. Their marching an unmilitary compromise: short step, short swing. Heeling. A practice kick: double, triple, in unison, the five of them. Unison. Precision.

They knock down a boy who is in their way. They surround him. They make dangerous kicks at him. Erotokritou perhaps inadvertently kicks his elbow. The boy is in great pain.

"What d'you lot think you're doing?" Albert says.

"Practisin'."

"We're the Corps."

"You'll all be corpses right enough if you carry on like this," Albert says, failing to resist the chance of the pun provided by the pronunciation.

"Yeah, yeah?"

"You and who?"

"You watch it, Albie!"

"What did you say?" Albert says.

"Nothing!"

"He din't say nothin'!"

"You bin sayin' fings about ma famly?"

"You say 'sir' if you've anything to say to me," Albert says.

"Since when was you knighted by the Queen, then?"

"All right, then, that's your break. All of you, upstairs and stand outside the Headmaster's room," Albert says.

"After break, Albie."

"When we finished practisin'."

"You'll get yours, Albert, just you wait."

* * * * *

Terry was enjoying a *galatopoureko*: the membrane-thin flakes of pastry were crisp contrast to the yielding density of the centre, the honey ran with each bite.

Albert sat, within himself, quite alone. His shattered state after each school day seemed to last longer and longer: soon it would be permanent, he felt, in spite of the end of term being near.

"They tell me," he said to Terry, who did not listen, "that the kids take breaking up rather literally. Violently. Especially the kids who are leaving. Last term windows were broken and a couple of doors kicked in, and a lot of them brought booze in the afternoon. And the teachers had to go home in groups. Not that the kids couldn't tackle groups, though, for they could, easily enough. Did I tell you about this street fight with the Hoxton boys the other afternoon? They finish fifteen minutes before us, so that just gives them nice time to get up to us. One of the senior teachers heard there was going to be trouble, so he told the Head. You know what the old sod did? He said as it was going to be outside the school it was none of his business! None of his business! Eventually he was persuaded to phone the police about it, however, and they had a car out-side at four-ten. But they couldn't do anything. The fight still happened. The police just aren't a deterrent to these kids, there's no deterrent that I know of. Anything they want to do, they do. And somehow I've got to admire them for it, even though I seem to be on the other side. Some-how they're behaving more like human beings than we are. It's the authority which is wrong, not those it's forced upon. People like the bloody Head and this inspector who came yesterday. She came into my class just as I'd got them under, which takes about ten minutes, and after a bit she asked me if she could take over. I was only too pleased to be shown how to deal with them, of course. 'You're too tense, all of you,' she says. 'Relax, look, go floppy, like this, go floppy.' My class went floppy all right, all over the place, and the noise! She just walked out after a few minutes, the cow, and I had to go round calming them down with my special foreknuckle headrap. That's the sort of authority I mean, hers, that's all wrong. It must be all wrong. Or I'm mad, which is after all not impossible."

Georgiou's latest waitress came to stack and pick up the cups and plates.

"Give with the reechy kisses, babe," said Albert.

"Kindly get stuffed," said the waitress.

"Only time I did touch them, hurt them," Albert resumed, "was today, for the first time. I was giving a bloody brilliant lesson on architecture—it was brilliant, too—and the bastards still weren't paying attention and still mucked about, and I lost my temper and said they were a lot of peasants. That they resented, being called peasants, that touched them, that hurt them. They copied chunks out of the Bible for the rest of the lesson, and I could feel the resentment in the room. It wasn't the copying out of the Bible, I'm sure, they probably hated that less than me rabbeting on about architecture, but being called peasants. Perhaps it has country bumpkin associations for London kids. Strange that it should be the only thing to touch them. But you know what I've decided to do in the last few days of term? I'm going to give them time and paper to write down exactly what they feel about me, with a guarantee that there will be no complaints or recriminations from me, whatever they say. This I hope will work out their hatred of me without it actually needing to come to violence. How about that for an idea, then?"

* * * * *

Cablestrasse

The Blue Angel had changed. I noticed the door was set differently as soon as I went through it. But the football machine was the same, the room was the same. The barman was different. He sat on two tables, stretched, and did not seem inclined to serve. Got stickybun for self, coffee for all, including mate from very posh bank (Coutts? Higginson?) just picked up in pub. Played football with him. Drunken negro kept saying fuck; reproved him for it. Beat posh mate twice. Then stood aside, inviting Terry to play with him. Terry kept popping outside, would not play. Giant negro gets up, offers to play posh mate; does so. I stand eating me stickybun, one foot on a chair, as is my wont. Older negro comes up and asks me to put me foot down. D'you own the joint then? I ask. Don't ask no questions, he says. Don' ask no questions! says giant negro. I'll ask what fucking questions I fucking like, I says, with which he hits me on chest, half-caught blow on hand, did not hurt, but I knocked my right shin on the chair and my head against the wall. Luckily his mates held him back after that—but he kept on saying things like Let me cut him down to size. I put me foot up again and went on eating me bun. Older mate again said Put it down! And Giant seemed about to get loose, so I glared at the lot, threw me bun down violently and exited.

Outside found by Terry. Walked down NE Passage. Told him about it. Gave me benefit of his fighting experience. Went back, to another, cellar, one. Giant came in after we had been there a few minutes and Terry making up to girl, dancing. Decided to leave after a couple of nother minutes. Walked, came back, telling Terry man who hit me was down there. Were standing at cellar door, packed, too to go in. Saw Giant negro other side of room. Narrowed me eyes at him. He came storming across room shouting I'll kill the bastard! I belted up stairs, waited at top to see if he was coming. He was, screaming something I don't remember. I screamed something back that included fuck and indicated he wouldn't be able to do it; and ran through passage into street. Stood outside, feeling fairly safe, but elated, shitscared, waiting for Terry. He came out after a couple of minutes, saying he had held negro at bottom of stairs so's he couldn't get up, blocking way up. He and others. Thanked him.

While we stood outside, pro passed and was in a scuffle. Police van immediately drew up, six or eight coppers got out and shoved someone in; negro. Pro shouting He tried to roll me! Take him in! I won't let any one roll me! Saw Terry and me and warned us against trying to roll her, as well. Another pro came up and talked with us about her—said she was a horrible woman. Gathered first pro was trying to muscle in on the Strasse.

Stood there a long time. Man who hit me came out, looked at us both, and went other way. Terry had meanwhile talked me into feeling safe and not running farther. Not that I didn't feel shitscared all the time, but that I accepted it and would have fought, I think, if occasion had arisen. Pro who had been rolled came back past us, on own. Terry just stepped out in front of her, and looked down at her. She apologised! Terry stepped back. Terry really rather magnificent the whole evening. Told to move on by two highup police in car.

Went down by bombed buildings, following quarrelling pro and ponce. (Earlier had thrown two milk bottles, one each, into playground in middle of Wellclose Square; Terry's broke, mine did not; can't even rely on laws of physics, now, I said bitterly.) Saw whole row of milk bottles. Did not pick them up—luckily, for policeman just farther on talking to drunk leaning over wall. Went on. Suddenly had an epiphany on sight of the roofline (*it hit me, it hit me: someone, some people, humankind, had thought about that roofline, had conceived it; it wasn't brilliant, or graceful, it was just of humankind, man's, sweated from his conscious*) and stopped to write it down. Policeman caught up with us, asked what I had in my hand, what my address was. Questioned his right to ask me anything. Terry warning me not to be awkward. Young copper, not a Londoner—Yorkshire? Showed him piece of paper—much good would it do him. Satisfied. Went up towards Wellclose Square again—Terry pissed through wire fence opposite spaghetti works. Just as I was following him, copper on bike came by. Went past, but somehow we knew he'd stopped. So we played with him up towards the Sq., dodging in and out of doorways, he following very slowly on his bike. I found a paperclip in my doorway. Did not follow us right into sq. Leaned against lampost in sq, saw copper move on couple of women and man, drunk, laughing. Copper came up to us. What were we doing. I was just standing quietly talking to my mate about the architecture, I says, they're very nice late eighteenth-century houses over there. Very reasonable copper. Not narked. Just said not the time to appreciate architecture, as this was Stepney and any minute a drunken man might rush out of a house with a knife in his hand and stick it into the first person he saw; who might well be me.

*   *   *   *   *

On the thirtieth of May, he was at Eleanour Bull's on Deptford Strand, with three men: Poley, Skeres, and Frizer. Poley was in the service of Elizabeth's government as a courier; Skeres was a government spy; little is known of Frizer. It was Frizer who had invited him to Deptford.

They met at about ten in the morning, and after lunch talked quietly together and walked in the garden of the place until about six in the evening. They then returned to the same room to dine.

After the meal he began a quarrel with Frizer over the reckoning. He was lying on a bed, and Frizer was sitting on a chair with his back to him, between Poley and Skeres. From malice and what Kyd called "his rashnes in attempting soden pryuie iniuries to men", he drew Frizer's knife and gave him two scalp wounds. Frizer, in defending himself, struggled to take back his knife, and inflicted on him a mortal wound above his right eye (the blade penetrating to a depth of two inches) from which he died instantly. Christopher Marlowe, Poet, February 1564 to May 1593.

* * * * *

What I think of flabby Chops Albert

Sir you get on any ones nerrves. with all you'r rules. regala-
tions. you say you are not allowed to talk in class but you
are not allowed to canne you you have canned me and
others You like to take the mick out of people yet if we
take the mick out of you you start being a bully. you enjoy
hiting us you don't care if we don't do any thing you still
hit us, like yesterday when you hit us for cheering you did
not know who cheered and who didn't. I myself saw a girl
cheer. In taking the mick you couldn't touch your Hair
with a pair of garden Shears with out a lot of trouble you'r
and proper pleasent your' self

English
Composition
on
What I think of Albert

I think Albert is a very nice teacher, but I dont like the
way he shout at the students and clout the boys on their
head. He is a teacher of great knowledge and very polite.
I know some times the children gets on his nerves. But I
think two boys, he should clout is Franco and Turk. I am
very clad he hasen hit the girls, because his hands might
mist and hit them in the wrong place, Albert has fair hair
hanging over his face, he is kind of fatish has blue eyes. I
think he teaches very good and I know he tries his best
that all about you

Albert   the end.

English

I think Mr Albert on the whole is a good teacher and I have learned a lot with him. But at times he runs round the classroom like a <u>manaic</u>, and clumps anyone in range of his hand, when he hits some boys around the head it give them a head-ache. He I think is trying to get thinner because he bealts around classroom. He should at the end of the week have a hair-cut, he is always pushing his hair back.

My Definition of Mr Albert

MR ALBERT HAS A POOR OUTLOOK TOWARDS US, CALLING US PEASANTS AND OTHER INSULTING NAMES OF WHICH WE WOULD LIKE TO CONTRADICT, IN OTHER WORDS TO CALL HIM A LIAR!

MR ALBERT ON THE WHOLE ALTHOUGH HE ISN'T ALL THERE IS A ROTTON TEACHER BUT NOT PROFFESSIONALLY FOR HE TEACHES WELL AND I AM GLAD HE IS IN MY GROUP OR SHOULD IT BE VICE VERSA. IN SCHOOL MR ALBERT IS AN AUTHENTIC NIT.

Yours sincerely
AN ADMIRER

Mr Albert

Is not to bad for teaching English and for haveing a little lark. but he is a big fat nits how is hiting Franco and Turky he is a bit hive on his fee Mr Albert wigha about 17 st 6 lb, when Mr Albert gets on a speaking wight mankin the mankin say get off you will break me in three

Mr Albert

Mr Albert is alright sometimes, but he gets very anoyed at us and shouts and calls us peasants and he goes round hitting people for nothing he only hits the boys so I'm glad I am not a boy.

He is very morbid and gross and he thinks that everybody is seducing him.

Mr Albert

I think mr Albert is Very Good teacher sod
I like him everybody does he is Very nice and fat he is
Very

I think mr Albert is a very spiteful teacher and he always moaaning. He always shout at the Student and clout the boys and the head. I think he is very polite any way. Any way think mr Alburt is nice other wise but only think he must not keep on punching the boys on the head for nothing some time the girls need one as well as the boys to Bring back there head to gether. Mr Albert always tell you off you cannot say nothing un less he tell you off or move from your seat and put you be side the Boys and I dont like that be cause I dont like Boys and I dos'nt sit be side my Brother. Franco is playing campion in class he want to Beat the Boys and girl in the class room But he cant do that to me be cause I am not a fraid of him he walk all about and hit Turce and hold him a his throat

and I dont like that so could you please tell him not to
do it for me please sir thank you very much. Mr Albert is
like to clout he people to much.

How I think of Mr. Albert

I think Mr. Albert is horrible sometimes because he is
allways morneing you can never say any think without get
told of or getting moved somewhere elese. Mr Albert is
fat and has fair hair, he allways has a joke with the boys
but never with the girls because he's to morney. He is not
a bit moden he wears old fashion round toe shoes baggy
trouser and a dirty looking tie. His hair is always over the
place, any body would think he has't got a comb. I think
he is bit spitefull to the boys just because they say something silly but some do need hiting but not on the head.
He is not very strice, when he its a boy and the boy startes
sobbing or answering him back he gets scared and starts
being nice to the boy. if a person stays away the next time
he or she comes back he asked what they away for and
that is being nosey and its nun of his bisness he to nosey.
He's always got some one to shout at and when he does
shout you would think the building was caveing in. it is
not feare the he should only split the girls up but not the
boys.

Mr ALBERT. I like mr Albert sometimes when he is in a
good mood But when he isint I don't like him and I don't
like him when he tells us to writh or Read, and I don't like

him when he hits me and when he calls me nams his all
fat and no bone he has a Bannor nose, and we know he
can't play the Panio, sometimes he says he 7000 years <u>old</u>
and sometimes he says he 1400 years <u>old</u>. I feel sorry
for Mr Albert because we all knows he is <u>Round the Bend</u>
and a Bit rusty Still nevery midd a, and and he in love
with Gloria Haper and Jean Tig and he has been married
ten times and he is quite small, and he is not very strick.
and he is a Bossy no Good lay about nut case, I bet he
Perms his hair Everynight and I say him do the v sign and
he is a holargan and he says things about our family and
our Grandmars.

Our Techerer
Mr ALBERT

He is rather a nice person to talk too he lets you do what
you wante if hes in a good mood he rams his gob like he is
soposed two and ceeps his place don get out of hand he
is nown by som of the Boy's Mick Norm Anglei and
mayself <u>CHAS</u> as poulong the pourden i think he trise his
hardest But i think he has a bit more go in him but he
dont want to yuse it on us he is quite tall and on the plup
side But i cant tallk somtimes when we all sit down to
work and he sets us the Boy's including me just fuk about
in class and take the mike out of him we also somtimes just
take no notis and just carey on withe what we are dowing
somtimes i think he must fell like just droping avver thing
and give up but he just perseyveres,

MR Albert

MR Albert is a very good sports because he can take a joke. He is allways separation me and Gloria and none of the boys. he is allways jokeing with the boys and not with the girl he think we are a bitter of dirty. I think he is

What I think of Mr. Alburt (SNOTY-NOSE)

I think Mr Alburt is a big fat over fed fool, and he dosn't teach us anything. But he can be alright when he wants to. When he calls us pesants I feel like booting him in the ear-hole. And when he hits us I feel like calling him dirty name and swearing at him. Also when he starts shouting his head of I feel like saying "Shut up you big fat lolop, and you fat barrel of compost. When we read that book I feel like raming it down his throat. Somtimes he says we are suducing him, but I would not like to suduce him for a start. When we go out the front and lean on hes piano he says, "Get off my piano," and ef he wasn't a teacher I would say Shut up Alburt and stick your piano right up your Kyber Pars. And what makes me wild is that he always picks on Turk the littlest boy in the class, one day I wish Turkey would turn round and gob in his eye. And yesterday when he was going out of the door a number of us started cheering, so he imeadiately hit all the boys, but I saw two girls cheering also. But if you told him he would say shut up and go away. I also don't like his type of music he favorite composer is Back and he is a right berk to. The other day we had Beethoven and we started calling he pieces of music Beethoven blues and Snoty Olivers' Symphony in Z+. And when he plays other sort of music he goes all funny and starts whistling, and makes out he's a conductor, <u>LIKE A BIG FAT OVER-FED NITT.</u>

He is orable for one thing for a nother he is a nosens
His face is like a back of a bus.
His to big for his boots
He is a bit of a film Star he acted the part of Garula.
He walks like a firy elephant.
We all call him puw long of the elephant.
He has got hire like a goly-wog
All the clouth he wers are from the rag shop
I wouldnot say wot I think of him in publick.
But he is a good OLD?
His diner is to big for his stomoc
he is related to a elephant I think.
But relly he is a ?
Evry time he gets on the scals the scals say one at a time.
or no elephant alowd.
       THAT IS THE END OF GOLDY-LOX

What I think of Mr. Albert

I think Mr. Albert is a peasant. For I beilieve it takes a peasant to know another peasant. Mr Albert is a great big muscle-bound bully. I put him in the same catogary as Hitler and Mussilinea. Mr. Albert looks posativly stupid having his hair long and bushy and having it over his eyes.

So that every so often he has to push his hiar out of his eyes. This is very distracting when reading a look. But his choice of books are terrible, borring, unexciting and when Mr. Albert reads the noise, is borring and at least five times while Mr. Albert was reading I nearly fell asleep.

9 lessons out of ten he gives writting.

I think he is a fat, porky selfish drip.

AND HOW ! ! ! ! ! ! ! !

MR. Alburt

I think that mr. Alburt is the worse teacher in the school. He is a bully and he think's he is Mr. Alburt 1963. He also could do with a lawn mower over his head, in other words he has got enough hair on his head to stuff a suite of furniture, in simple words he needs an hair-cut. He is the most unsuting teacher you could ever get, he calls us peasents beacuse he thinks we are like himself. Myself I think his a bit gone in his head. And my finale words are I wish he would go and decay.

P.S.

I think he's a big Nancy.

What I think of mr Alburt

I think that you are horrible you always go round the class hitting us and also shout at us as if we were fools like you. you're a big fat lolop and you also are mad. You never give us hard work We are always writing essays and reading you are the fattest teacher in the school but you can also be good at times and could be the best teacher in the school you big fat nit. Slobbery Jew you fat fomf you soppy rabbi. you are a dog. ON THE WHOLE YOUR STUPID AND YOU ARE A FAT FOMF OXEN NIT LOLOP RABBI FART-FACE.

Mr. Albert

I think you are a man who likes hitting children and kicking there behinds. You calls us 'peasants I say you are a big fat peasant and a fatty lamb chop, You goe in public houses nearly every night. You ought to hang yourself or Commit suicide in the River Thames Your a bloody nuisance a big Head. Its a wonder your still alive or otherwise you would be dead and buried, like many of us wish you to be. You look like mussllinea and goldy laks. Your a great big fat kick donkey, you talk of us you haven't looked at your self properly. Your hair is all over the place and like a poodle who hasn't had hes hair clipped. Your like a Ape or a fully grown chimpanzee like in the book, when he gave him a bottle of beer to drink he got drunk and it took ages to Sober him up, I should think it takes more than a few hours to sober you up after finishing with the pubs.

What I think of mr Albert

I think mr Albert is a good teacher sometimes what i like about him is he gives a lot of work sometimes he gets to big for his boots he jumps on kids for nothing. Someday good old mr Albert will come a cross someone his own Size who will splatter him to bits and pices he gives us good lessons sometimes i feel like swearing at him but still he's a good English teacher. There's on thing wrong with him he needs a haricut. And one thing more he rekcons his self to much he gose round the class punching us for nothing and on Friday night I am going to break his Stick. And I next term he better not go round the class hiting us for nothing like he dos'e NOW for his sake. I admitt me Chas, Mick, Norm, are troble makers but a least we don't do it for troble we do it for fun as a lot of other kids do i be glad when we brake up for summer hoildays to get away from all the teachers.

*   *   *   *   *

After fifteen hours of rain, in the late afternoon the sun slashed through, lightening first over the south-westward houses of the Circus, glinting silver on the wet courses of the chimneys and throwing the dormers into shadowed mystery. A patterned flight of sparrows was scattered in reflection from the polished roof of a car outside.

Albert lazed at his drawingboard before the great window. Nearly seven weeks' summer holiday lay ahead of him in which to work; and he could not work today, always tomorrow was the day he was going to work. Part of the trouble, he thought, was that he lived and loved to live in an area of absolute architectural rightness, which inhibited his own originality, and resulted in him being—— OH, FUCK ALL THIS LYING!

FOUR: Disintegration

——fuck all this lying look what im really trying to write about is writing not all this stuff about architecture trying to say something about writing about my writing im my hero though what a useless appellation my first character then im trying to say something about me through him albert an architect when whats the point in covering up covering up covering over pretending pretending i can say anything through him that is anything that I would be interested in saying

——so an almighty aposiopesis

——Im trying to say something not tell a story telling stories is telling lies and I want to tell the truth about me about my experience about my truth about my truth to reality about sitting here writing looking out across Claremont Square trying to say something about the writing

and nothing being an answer to the loneliness to the lack
of loving

———look then I'm

———again for what is writing if not truth my truthtelling
truth to experience to my experience and if I start falsify-
ing in telling stories then I move away from the truth of
my truth which is not good oh certainly not good by any
manner of

———so it's nothing

———look, I'm trying to tell you something of what I feel
about being a poet in a world where only poets care anything real about poetry, through the objective correlative
of an architect who has to earn his living as a teacher.
this device you cannot have failed to see creaking, ill-
fitting at many places, many places, for architects *manqués*
can earn livings very nearly connected with their art, and
no poet has ever lived by his poetry, and architecture has
a functional aspect quite lacking in poetry, and, simply,
architecture is just not poetry.

———In a world which offers nothing but hardly-con-
nected substitutes to keep me being a poet tomorrow; not
that I am complaining, you should understand this, being
a poet today is the only reason necessary to want to be a
poet tomorrow; but I am concerned to tell you something
of what this means, of what I think it means, in the living,
as well as I can, I have to write, I have to tell the truth, it's
compulsive, yet at the same time agonising, to write to pass
the time I have too much of, of which I have too much, the

end can't come quickly enough for me, as long as I don't actually have to do anything about it, but meanwhile I have to write something, to pass the time, being interested in so much, everything really, everything, compulsively, *nihil humanum a me alienum puto* and all that jazz.

———So it's nothing to you that I am rabbeting on about being a poet and having to earn a living in other ways: but what about your own sector of the human condition then? Eh? Eh? Eh eh eh!

———It is about frustration.

———The poetry comes from the suffering. The poetry is the only thing to make me face the further suffering. For the poetry any suffering is endurable. Even years for a single line.

———Is too

———Is about the fragmentariness of life, too, attempts to reproduce the moment-to-moment fragmentariness of life, my life, and to echo it in technique, the fragmentariness, a collage made of the fragments of my own life, the poor odds and sods, the bric-à-brac, a thing composed of, then.

———Tell me a story, tell me a story. The infants.

———Not that I am not fond of Albert, for I am, very; Albert, a slightly comic association with the name, offset today, as a name, and Albert Albert, to emphasize his Albertness, hisness, itness, uniqueness, yes, fond of him, I am, very, even though I have hardly provided you with a description of him, a corporate being, I know, but he stands for me, I don't need one: Albert, who stands for me, poor fool.

——And also to echo the complexity of life, reproduce some of the complexity of selves which I contain within me, contradictory and gross as they are: childish, some will call it, peeing in the rainfall gauge, yes, but sometimes I am childish, very, so are we all, it's part of the complexity I'm trying to reproduce, exorcise.

——Faced with the enormous detail, vitality, size, of this complexity, of life, there is a great temptation for a writer to impose his own pattern, an arbitrary pattern which must falsify, cannot do anything other than falsify; or he invents, which is pure lying. Looking back and imposing a pattern to come to terms with the past must be avoided. Lies, lies, lies. Secondbest at best, for other writers, to do them a favour, to give them the benefit of innumerable doubts.

——Faced with the enormity of life, all I can do is to present a paradigm of truth to reality as I see it: and there's the difficulty: for Albert defecates for instance only once during the whole of this book: what sort of a paradigm of the truth is that?

——Further, since each reader brings to each word his own however slightly different idiosyncratic meaning, how can I be expected to make my own—but you must be tired.

——On then to talk of Jenny, Jenny, a name I like even though originally I intended it to be involved in a rather coarse pun, Jenny Taylor, Jenny Taylor, I've had no girl called Jenny, whereas hers was Muriel, which even before I knew her I thought comic, now I hate it, you can't call a girl in a book Muriel, now can you? And not a cripple but an epileptic, he was, her earlier lover, with whom I could not compete, being whole. But Balgy, Balgy, the name I kept, from some oddness, though it is in Scotland, not Ireland, on the southern shore of Loch Torridon; not that I could remember much about what it looked like, I had to pinch the scenery, such as it is, for that section, from North Wales, which I know much better.

——That's the trouble, I don't remember anything like everything, or even enough, so in writing about it I'm at a disadvantage straight away, really, trying to put down what is true. In asking Frank, for instance, what he could remember of what I had said to him when I came back from Balgy, he said the only thing I mentioned was that I had noticed that she did not wash as often as I had felt was consonant with my own surely not excessive practice.

——But an effect, salutary, yes, it has had, this working out things with her under the name of Jenny, of release, a definite effect of release, though I think it may be coincidental, really, or at best only contributory. But welcome, nevertheless, having been held in this memory's thrall these four and a half years, to be released, being by the end of this book not under the influence of her memory, suffering the pain of her betrayal, as I was at its beginning.

——Not that most of it was not fantasy, in the first place, of course, for it was: if I had really wanted her all those years I should have gone out and found her again, have

made her mine, have made her want me. It was the fantasy
that had to be broken. Fantasy on my part, deception on
hers. For it was I who actually broke from her, wanting
too much, and her not giving, or being unable to give, she
put me in a position where I had to break away, to nurse
my fantasy without its being broken by her reality, and in
this I was grievously wrong, to myself, and to her, self-
delusion is the worst crime.

——So that's another shifting of reality, in the course of
the book I've come to see differently events I believed to
be fixed, changed my mind about Muriel, I have this other
girl, Virginia, now, at the time of writing, very happy too,
but who knows what else will have shifted by galleyproof
stage, or pageproof stage, or by publication day, or by the
time you are reading this? Between writing and galleys,
they've cut down some of the trees in Percy Circus, for
another instance, taken down the railings, you'll just have
to take my word for the description, now, now all I can say
is That's how it was, then, that's the truth.

——But it is good that I am rid of the ghost of Muriel,
have laid her ghost, difficult to lay, a ghost, good to be rid
of the using her as an excuse for not loving, for not giving
to, anyone else, good to be able to try now to build a new
relationship on truth, no fantasy as to the kind of person . . .
enough of this emotional sewerage.

——A few instances of the lies. It was Jim Wales not
Wells kept the greyhounds; my parents used to live in
Hammersmith but now live in Barnes; the Little Heathens
I pinched from my father but gave the whippety player
his name in payment, in slight recompense; and my parents

have two cats, not one dog, who eat nourishing Fidomeat, not Felixmeat, which I made up, yes, I'm guilty, I made that word up; and I am unjust to my parents; and she had a broken not a hooked nose; and it is a Morris Minor not a Fiat we park in Wellclose Square; and at Balgy I drank loch water, not her, and we read poems, not designed a house, and she sketched but not me, who could never sketch, nor draw, nor paint; and only once we bathed in the pool, and it was very cold, I only went in to the waist, and she hardly more, and it was very cold, and we dressed again as quickly as possible, and sat and shivered; even Littlewoods I changed to Woolworths; and . . . I could go on and on, through each page, page after page, pointing out the lies, the lies, but it would be so tedious, so tedious.

———And even old Charlie, had to change his name to Georgie, dreadful name, as well, for god knows why, to say nothing of his wife: I went into the pub the other day, and Bert said, Remember Charlie's wife? Yes, I said. Dead and buried, he said, dead and buried. So there you are: let her epitaph be 𝕯𝖎𝖊𝖉 𝖇𝖊𝖋𝖔𝖗𝖊 𝕴𝖓𝖈𝖔𝖗𝖕𝖔𝖗𝖆𝖙𝖎𝖔𝖓. You just can't keep up with it, life.

———The one I feel sorry for is little Linda Taylor, made an epileptic, to suit my ends, the poor little figment.

———And oh but what other material is not now to be worked in! The visit to Zulf, for instance, who lives over-looking a cemetery and diverts Albert with detailed descriptions of the Week's Burials; the teacher who sleeps in the woodwork shed and cooks over the gluepot gasring; Albert playing the identities game at St. Pancras Station to first the bewilderment and then the anger of a rozzer;

the story of the child who cooked her newborn and un-
wanted baby in her publican father's salmon kettle, the
better to cut up and dispose of it: the Quixotian Adventure
of the Coloured Bird.

——And what of the projected scene in which Miss
Crossthwaite was to have been set upon by a group of
ruffianly and sensually-intent schoolboys? Left undone,
undone, Marlene left unmauled.

——But here's another story, to help to make up for
your disappointment, one story for another. There was this
man, see (there's always this man), there was this man, an
Arab, if you like, driving a coachload of bints through the
desert, for days and days—five days, if you like, and every
time one of the bints—they were wearing yashmaks and
whatevers, and were all pure and holy, undefiled and
virgin, if you like, every time one of the bints heard a call
of nature they'd make him, this driver, stop, and they'd all
form a ring around her so's she couldn't be seen, in the
desert, except for a couple who would keep an eye on this
driver, like. So I mean, he stuck the first day out with mere
fortitude, and the second day with the blessing of a
bladder of quite unique and hitherto unsuspected capacity.
But on the third day, still driving across the desert, still
unable to relieve himself as a result of the undefiled nature
of his charges, for the third day unable—when suddenly,
suddenly: he sees a lone Arab approaching on a camel. In
the middle of the desert, this is, you remember. So, our
driver, unable to contain himself any longer, and taking
the bints by surprise for the first time, stops the coach,
leaps out, locks the door behind him, runs to the man on
the camel and says, panting: Allah be with you, o fortu-

nately encountered one, can you tell me where I may purchase a score of white horses? And the man on the camel replies, Indeed, this is a fortunate meeting, o driver of innumerable bints, for only three miles to the south dwells my brother Fazeem, who has a hundred of the whitest horses in the whole of Arabia, horses of such pure breeding that men seek them from all parts of the world, and when the moon shines on their flanks then they gleam white like newdrawn milk. Thank you, said the bintdriver, and tell me, o rarely mounted one, if you can, where I may find twenty black horses that I might purchase? Allah must indeed, said the cameldriver, have contrived this encounter, o driver of a handsome vehicle, for only some nine miles to the east dwells my cousin Hamid, who has a stable of such black horses the equal of those white horses of my brother Fazeem, black horses of such rarity and comeliness that when the allseeing moon shines on their flanks it is as though it glinted on the finest Damascus steel. Allah be praised, said the driver, o one dressed in comely raiment, and can you tell me where I can buy piebald horses? This day Allah has indeed excelled himself in felicity, o preoccupied one, indeed, for only five miles to the east is the house of my second cousin Abdul, who has taken the milkwhite stallions of my brother Fazeem and the steelblack mares of my cousin Hamid and has produced piebald horses of such quality to be seen nowhere else in all the world, and when the—— Here, mate, what's that you're doing up against my camel's leg?

——And another of my aims is didactic: the novel must be a vehicle for conveying truth, and to this end every device and technique of the printer's art should be at the command of the writer: hence the future-seeing holes, for instance, as much to draw attention to the possibilites as to make my point about death and poetry.

———A page is an area on which I may place any signs I consider to communicate most nearly what I have to convey: therefore I employ, within the pocket of my publisher and the patience of my printer, typographical techniques beyond the arbitrary and constricting limits of the conventional novel. To dismiss such techniques as gimmicks, or to refuse to take them seriously, is crassly to miss the point.

———Didactic, too, social comment on teaching, to draw attention, too, to improve: but with less hope, for if the government wanted better education it could be provided easily enough, so I must conclude, again, that they specifically want the majority of children to be only partially-educated.

———Oh, and there were some pretty parallels to be drawn between built-on-the-skew, tatty, half-complete, comically-called Percy Circus, and Albert, and London, and England, and the human condition.

———"I, yeoman and churchwarden of this parish these thirty years, have seen and had a hand in some doings hereabouts, and if anybody cares to read a simple tale simply told then they can. . . ."

———Go elsewhere for their lies. Life is not like that, is just not like that.

———But even I (even I!) would not leave such a mess, such a mess, so many loose ends, clear up the mess, bury the loose ends, the lot. . . .

FIVE: Coda

FIVER Code

Night. A group of five marched west up Vincent Terrace
along by the canal. Albert walked south along Colebrooke
Row across and above the canal tunnel entrance.

"It's Albie."

"From the Angel. Well, well."

"Yeah yeah!"

"Albert Angelo."

"Ma famly?"

"Right!—One! Two!   Three!"

"Ma! Fam! Leeeeeee!"

"Ouuuugh!"

"United by the Queen, the bastard!"

"Sir! Sir!   Sir!"

"Right!—Up!"

"And over!"
" 'E'll roll, all right, fatarse Albert."

Hardly a splash.

*   *   *   *   *

A funeral is rather a nastey thing it allways makes me come
out in goospimples and all cold when i herd my big sisters
friends mama pastaway She said to us whould you like to
see the body at first my mother would not let us then she
went and see it buy urself when she come home she sade
it was a nastey sight to see she said that the bodey was all
painted up gust like somone on the stage thay panted the
lips more red and the face hes pink and yellow thaye say it
proseves it bus i think its Just plan stupid two spend and
wast all that money on a thing like that it was Just a gerate
wast of time and all that work fore relley nothing Just a
shocking display of funeralization on behaf of the furm
that was calld in.